THE TOP-SECRET ADVENTURE OF JOHN DARRAGH,

REVOLUTIONARY WAR SPY

BY **PETER ROOP** AND **CONNIE ROOP**
ADAPTED BY **AMANDA DOERING TOURVILLE**
ILLUSTRATED BY **ZACHARY TROVER**

Graphic Universe™ Minneapolis • New York

INTRODUCTION

SPIES PLAYED AN IMPORTANT ROLE IN THE REVOLUTIONARY WAR
(1775-1783). AMERICAN SPIES KEPT GENERAL GEORGE WASHINGTON
INFORMED ABOUT THE SIZE OF THE BRITISH ARMIES AND THE STATE
OF THEIR SUPPLIES. SPIES OFTEN DISCOVERED WHEN AND WHERE
THE BRITISH PLANNED TO ATTACK.

IN THE FALL OF 1777, THE BRITISH ARMY, UNDER THE COMMAND OF
GENERAL WILLIAM HOWE, HAD CAPTURED AND OCCUPIED PHILADELPHIA,
PENNSYLVANIA. THE DARRAGH FAMILY LIVED ACROSS THE STREET
FROM GENERAL HOWE'S BRITISH HEADQUARTERS. THE DARRAGHS
WERE QUAKERS. THEY USED THE WORDS *THEE, THY,* AND *THOU* WHEN
THEY SPOKE TO EACH OTHER. THEY OPPOSED VIOLENCE. THEY WERE
NOT SUPPOSED TO FIGHT ON EITHER SIDE. BUT CHARLES, THE OLDEST

DARRAGH SON, HAD JOINED GENERAL WASHINGTON'S ARMY, WHICH WAS ENCAMPED SOME DISTANCE OUTSIDE THE CITY. THE REST OF THE FAMILY BECAME SPIES TO HELP KEEP CHARLES SAFE.

MR. DARRAGH, A TEACHER, CREATED A CODE FOR SECRET MESSAGES. MRS. DARRAGH HID THE MESSAGES IN THE BUTTONS OF HER SON JOHN'S COAT. FOURTEEN-YEAR-OLD JOHN THEN TOOK THE MESSAGES TO WASHINGTON'S CAMP, WHERE CHARLES DARRAGH READ THEM.

THIS STORY TELLS WHAT MIGHT HAVE HAPPENED ON ONE OF JOHN DARRAGH'S DANGEROUS MISSIONS AS AN AMERICAN SPY.

PHILADELPHIA, PENNSYLVANIA
AN AUTUMN MORNING
1777

JOHN KNEW THAT IF THE GUARDS FOUND HIM PAST HIS AUNT'S HOUSE, THEY WOULD GUESS THAT HE WAS A SPY.
I'M SURE TO RUN INTO MORE SOLDIERS. I MUST BE CAREFUL.

AFTERWORD

ALTHOUGH JOHN DARRAGH HELPED HIS PARENTS SPY ON THE BRITISH, HIS MOTHER, LYDIA, WOULD BECOME THE MOST FAMOUS SPY IN THE FAMILY. IN LATE 1777, THE DARRAGH FAMILY WAS FORCED TO HOUSE BRITISH SOLDIERS IN THEIR HOME. LYDIA SENT HER YOUNGEST CHILDREN TO STAY WITH RELATIVES SO THEY WOULD BE SAFE. ON DECEMBER 2, 1777, THE SOLDIERS HELD A PRIVATE MEETING IN THE DARRAGH HOME. LYDIA HID IN A CLOSET NEAR THE ROOM WHERE THE SOLDIERS WERE MEETING. SHE OVERHEARD PLANS FOR AN ATTACK ON AMERICAN FORCES ON DECEMBER 4.

LYDIA DECIDED TO DELIVER THE NEWS OF THE ATTACK HERSELF. SHE LEFT TOWN EARLY ON DECEMBER 4, CARRYING A PASS THAT ALLOWED HER TO VISIT HER CHILDREN. ON THE WAY, SHE MET AN AMERICAN OFFICER. SHE TOLD HIM ABOUT THE PLANNED ATTACK. THE OFFICER MADE SURE THE AMERICANS HAD TIME TO PREPARE FOR BATTLE. AFTER A FOUR-DAY STANDOFF, THE BRITISH RETREATED BACK TO PHILADELPHIA. AFTERWARD, THE BRITISH SUSPECTED SOMEONE—MAYBE LYDIA—HAD OVERHEARD THEIR PLANS. SHE TOLD THEM THAT SHE AND HER FAMILY HAD BEEN ASLEEP IN THEIR ROOMS THE ENTIRE NIGHT OF THE MEETING. THE BRITISH SOLDIERS BELIEVED HER, AND SHE AND HER FAMILY WERE NOT HARMED.

FURTHER READING AND WEBSITES

ALLEN, THOMAS B. *GEORGE WASHINGTON, SPYMASTER: HOW THE AMERICANS OUTSPIED THE BRITISH AND WON THE REVOLUTIONARY WAR.* WASHINGTON, DC: NATIONAL GEOGRAPHIC CHILDREN'S BOOKS, 2007.

THE AMERICAN REVOLUTION HOMEPAGE
HTTP://AMERICANREVWAR.HOMESTEAD.COM/FILES/INDEX2.HTM

COLONIAL GAMES AND TOYS
HTTP://NOAHWEBSTERHOUSE.ORG/GAMES.HTML

GEORGE WASHINGTON PICTURE GALLERY
HTTP://WWW.HISTORYPLACE.COM/UNITEDSTATES/REVOLUTION/WASH-PIX/GALLERY.HTM

LIBERTY'S KIDS COMPANION WEBSITE
HTTP://WWW.LIBERTYSKIDS.COM/

MILLER, BRANDON MARIE. *GEORGE WASHINGTON FOR KIDS: HIS LIFE AND TIMES WITH 21 ACTIVITIES.* CHICAGO: CHICAGO REVIEW PRESS, 2007.

NELSON, KRISTIN L. *THE WASHINGTON MONUMENT.* MINNEAPOLIS: LERNER PUBLICATIONS COMPANY, 2011.

PENNER, LUCILLE RECHT. *LIBERTY!: HOW THE REVOLUTIONARY WAR BEGAN.* NEW YORK: RANDOM HOUSE, 2002.

RANSOM, CANDICE. *GEORGE WASHINGTON.* MINNEAPOLIS: LERNER PUBLICATIONS COMPANY, 2002.

SWAIN, GWYNETH. *PENNSYLVANIA.* MINNEAPOLIS: LERNER PUBLICATIONS COMPANY, 2002.

WILLIAMS, JEAN KINNEY. *THE QUAKERS.* NEW YORK: FRANKLIN WATTS, 1998.

ABOUT THE AUTHORS

PETER ROOP AND CONNIE ROOP HAVE WRITTEN MANY BOOKS FOR CHILDREN. AS LONGTIME TEACHERS, THEY VALUE THE POWER OF WELL-WRITTEN STORIES THAT CAN INSPIRE THEIR READERS WITH THE NOTION THAT ANYTHING IS POSSIBLE. WHEN NOT TRAVELING WORLDWIDE OR SHARING THEIR LOVE OF READING AND WRITING IN SCHOOLS, THE ROOPS LIVE IN WISCONSIN.

ABOUT THE ADAPTER

AMANDA DOERING TOURVILLE HAS WRITTEN MORE THAN 40 BOOKS FOR CHILDREN. TOURVILLE IS GREATLY HONORED TO WRITE FOR YOUNG PEOPLE AND HOPES THAT THEY WILL LEARN TO LOVE READING AND LEARNING AS MUCH AS SHE DOES. WHEN NOT WRITING, TOURVILLE ENJOYS TRAVELING, PHOTOGRAPHY, AND HIKING. SHE LIVES IN MINNESOTA WITH HER HUSBAND AND GUINEA PIG.

ABOUT THE ILLUSTRATOR

ZACHARY TROVER HAS BEEN DRAWING SINCE HE WAS OLD ENOUGH TO HOLD A PENCIL AND HASN'T STOPPED YET. YOU CAN FIND HIM LIVING SOMEWHERE IN THE MIDWEST WITH HIS EXTREMELY PATIENT WIFE AND TWO EXTREMELY IMPATIENT DOGS.

Text copyright © 2011 by Lerner Publishing Group, Inc.
Illustrations © 2011 by Lerner Publishing Group, Inc.

Graphic Universe™ is a trademark of Lerner Publishing Group, Inc.

Graphic Universe™
A division of Lerner Publishing Group, Inc.
241 First Avenue North
Minneapolis, MN 55401 U.S.A.

Website address: www.lernerbooks.com

Library of Congress Cataloging-in-Publication Data

Roop, Peter.
    The top-secret adventure of John Darragh, Revolutionary War spy / by Peter Roop and Connie Roop ; adapted by Amanda Doering Tourville ; illustrator, Zachary Trover.
        p.   cm. — (History's kid heroes)
    Includes bibliographical references.
    ISBN: 978-0-7613-6174-9 (lib. bdg. : alk. paper)
    1. Darragh, John—Juvenile fiction. 2. United States—History—Revolution, 1775-1783—Juvenile fiction. 3. Graphic novels. [1. Graphic novels. 2. Darragh, John—Fiction. 3. United States—History—Revolution, 1775-1783—Fiction. 4. Spies—Fiction. 5. Quakers—Fiction. 6. Washington, George, 1732-1799—Fiction.] I. Roop, Connie. II. Tourville, Amanda Doering, 1980– III. Trover, Zachary, ill. IV. Title.
PZ7.7.R66Top 2011
973.3'85—dc22

2009051648

Manufactured in the United States of America
1—CG—7/15/10

HOW TO FIND
ANOTHER
HUSBAND

HOW TO FIND ANOTHER HUSBAND

...by someone who did

RUSTY ROTHMAN

 Cincinnati, Ohio

The Ann Landers column on page 177 appeared in the *Miami Herald,* and is used by permission of Ann Landers, News America Syndicate.

How to Find Another Husband . . . by someone who did.

Library of Congress Cataloging in Publication Data
Rothman, Rusty, 1930—
    How to find another husband—by someone who did.
    Bibliography: p.
    Includes index.
    I. Remarriage—United States. 2. Dating (Social customs) 3.
Mate selection—United States.
I. Title.
HQ1019.U6R67   1985   646.7'7   84-26925
ISBN 0-89879-176-6

Book design by Christine Aulicino.

To My Mother

Contents

Acknowledgments

WHEN I SET OUT to write the acknowledgments for this book, it started me thinking about my mother and her sisters, who raised their children and lived out their marriages through the Great Depression, the worst financial crisis this country has ever known. Even so, they always had room for an extra child or adult in their homes and their hearts, and they cooked and baked for weeks to make our birthdays, confirmations, graduations, and weddings into lifelong memories. With rare exceptions, their choices were limited. They never knew what it meant to go to a spa or to "do their own thing." They hardly ever left a bad marriage, postponed childbearing, went back to school, or sought a career. The fire of their unused potential fueled this project for me.

A number of other people made this book not only possible but in some cases easier, beginning with my first husband. Without that marriage I never would have finished my education, or have experienced the trauma of divorce and the challenge of returning to single life. My children—Leslie, Aimee, Wendy, and Cathy—have always supported me wholeheartedly and even assumed some of my responsibilities so that I could fulfill my personal needs after years of full-time mothering. During my divorce they never judged, criticized, or faltered in their love.

And then, of course, there is Leonard, my dear husband, who gave me the opportunity to write this book by marrying me and allowing me the time I needed to do it by his financial and emotional support. He was interested and encouraging at all stages of the project. Most of all, he didn't mind my exposing our relationship to you, the reader. This took guts and love—things he has plenty of.

There are also the people who encouraged me in the writing of the book itself. My gratitude to Milton Zatinsky, who originally suggested that I should write; to my cousin Bob Fendell, who provided writer-to-writer guidance; to Arthur Liebers, a professional writer who agreed to read, critique, and try to sell my original manuscript even though he didn't know me; to Richard Balkin, my agent, who sold the project and guided me on its presentation; to Carol Cartaino and Howard Wells, my editors at Writer's Digest Books, who consistently cooperated with me and encouraged me; to Catherine Shaw, the editor who patiently helped me clarify, organize, and crystallize my ideas into this format; and to my daughter Leslie, who helped with the typing of the final manuscript.

I also appreciated the facilities of the downtown branch of the Miami Public Library, and its efficient staff, who provided information with such consistent courtesy. The University of Miami Library was also indispensable to me in researching and writing this book. As an alumna I was proud of their impressive resources and their helpful attitude.

I don't know if other authors thank their home towns, but I love Miami and Miami Beach, where I live. As I sat at my typewriter, the bay sparkled outside my window, the boats cut their way along the water, and I could see the great cruise ships slip out toward the ocean. It nourished my soul when I looked at the natural beauty of this place, and gave me many moments of peace and tranquility during the struggle to put my thoughts on paper with some kind of meaning.

Last I want to thank the wonderful remarried men and women who shared their experiences with me, and my friends, especially Marilyn Lesser, Ph.D., who was always there to offer help and encouragement.

Rusty Rothman
Miami Beach, Florida
June 3, 1984

HOW TO FIND ANOTHER HUSBAND

Introduction

I FOUND ANOTHER HUSBAND and I was fifty-one years old! Not only that, but during the three years that I was single I had a marvelous time. I was rarely lonely, and had four quality relationships while I was flying solo. And I am not unique. This country is full of mature women who have had exciting romances, been pursued like schoolgirls, and then remarried under all kinds of circumstances. A sixty-two-year-old woman, widowed for the second time, recently told me about her second courtship and marriage to a wonderful man—proving that a woman of any age can find excitement and romance.

When I divorced my husband after a twenty-eight-year marriage, my friends regaled me with horror stories about the other middle-aged women they knew who had dared to leave the security of a marriage and to want "something more." But the yearning, striving part of me demanded more from life than I was getting—and so I left my marriage despite my fears. I know that many of you who read this book did not choose to be single again. You may have been widowed, or thought you had a happy marriage until your husband asked for a divorce. But we still have a lot in common. I, too, had to face life alone, so I can reassure you that you *can* enjoy your singlehood and find a new husband, just as I did.

I was one of those brides of the 1950s. I married at nineteen, never having lived anywhere but with my family, and thoroughly accepted the mentality of that era, which preached breeding, togetherness, and a retreat to the home. In other words, I lived a traditional life. My four daughters were delightful and my economic situation was not too bad, but I wasn't happy in my marriage and there was no place to go. My mother was dead, I had no money of my own, I had dropped out of college after one year, and my only work experience had been as a secretary for one year before I married. I didn't think it was possible for me to raise my four children alone, and in retrospect, I believe I was correct in that assumption.

I never really enjoyed such diversions as organization work, canasta, luncheons, and gossip. Every time I played cards, my mind wandered. I felt I should be somewhere else, *doing* something else, and that life was passing me by.

In 1964 my children were on their way to independence. My youngest child was in school, and I could see the rest of my life before me. It didn't look good. A new community college had opened up in Miami, so I decided to take some courses and try to finish my degree.

I was scared to death. Although I had been an honor student in high school, it had been seventeen years since my last classroom experience. I felt self-conscious being the only thirty-four-year-old in the classroom, but I loved it. I took one course at a time, going at night after the children were fed, bathed, and ready for bed. In 1969, after five years and two other universities, I earned my B.A. in psychology. My children were wonderful during those years, always supportive and cooperative.

The year I graduated, I got a job—my first—for the

State Division of Family Services, and used my earnings to pay for psychotherapy for myself. I knew I was going to therapy to find the strength to leave my husband, and I felt terribly guilty about it. But he knew I was unhappy in our marriage, and since he was not about to make any changes, I felt that it was up to me to make the move.

In 1970 I obtained a grant from our local Jewish Family Service Agency and started full-time graduate work for my master's degree in social work. It required two full years of intensive classroom training three days a week, plus work in an agency two days a week. Again, my children were very helpful and supportive, and never complained about my crazy schedule.

In 1972, after I graduated, I asked my husband for a divorce—but he became so upset by the idea of breaking up the family that I stayed in the marriage for six more years. By then, my youngest daughter was in her second year of college. No more excuses; I filed for divorce.

During this whole time I was working in my profession, first as a clinical social worker for the Dade County Alcohol Program and later as director of their Outpatient Treatment Center. My job required that I provide a great deal of group therapy, individual therapy, and program planning.

After my work for Dade County I went into private practice with a colleague. We founded a community counseling center, where we worked with people from all kinds of backgrounds and economic circumstances. Many of them were in the throes of divorce, thinking about divorce, or suffering from post-divorce adjustment problems.

During this time I became very interested in the lives of women in their middle years. I would often hear men speak of us as "neurotic," "menopausal," "depressive," "crazy," or suffering from the "empty nest syndrome." Meanwhile, all around me, I saw women in this age group holding down challenging, important jobs, looking great, doing interesting things, and heaving great sighs of relief when their children finally left home. At the same time I had the chance to observe my daughters and their female friends, all women in their twenties and thirties in the midst of *their* search for love and a commitment. So I was privy to the everyday problems and concerns of younger women as well, and I continued to read extensively on the subject of male/female relationships at every opportunity.

Both during and after my divorce, I took part in a divorce adjustment group attended by women and men of all ages, who had been single for varying periods of time. Later I taught similar classes for the YWCA and the local community college. I also had a lot of emotional support during my divorce; some professional, and a great deal from friends and family. But most important, I had a positive attitude, which drew people to me. I was hardly ever lonely—men and dates and friends sought me out. Those of you who are not single by choice will have to work on this positive attitude, and I will show you how.

After three years of happy singlehood I began to feel that I wanted another mate; it was then that I found one.

During my single years I spent many hours "rapping" with other single women about their fears, needs, and desires. The following pages contain a dialogue between myself and representative single women that I have known. The dialogue answers your questions about how to be happy as a single woman and how to find the man with whom you will share a new married life. These answers come from my professional experience as a social worker and psychotherapist, as well as from my personal experiences.

I also interviewed many successfully remarried women of all ages, and I include their advice too. They agree with me that men *are* available if you want a husband, and that it is really all right to want to be married instead of on your own. They also agree that the time *between* marriages can be an exciting and rewarding one for you.

This book takes an optimistic approach to the realities of being a single woman in today's world, and although it is not antithetical to the women's movement, it does advocate some feminine methods for getting your man. By "feminine" I simply mean feeling free to express your womanly qualities; I do not mean game playing, manipulation, or deceit. I have carefully researched the facts about marriage and remarriage, and have included them in the book to help you to decide whether you really want or need to marry again. Once you are sure that you want another husband, you can set out to do the job joyously, armed with knowledge—which we all know is power. As in any other endeavor, if you are well informed you will have the edge and accomplish your goal more readily. *This book is designed to give you that edge.*

CHAPTER ONE

Alone Again . . . And Liking It

So—you're alone. You may still be reeling from the divorce or death of your husband, or maybe you've been alone for some time now. You've had a taste of the impermanence of most things in life, and probably agree with Henry Miller that "the idea of permanence is an absurd illusion. Change is the most permanent thing you can say about the whole Universe."

You *know* that you will have to deal with life in one way or another. You are the master of your ship, and it is up to you to make the decisions that will affect the quality of the rest of your life. You can't avoid the responsibility. Even making no decision is a decision—you have decided not to decide!

The fact that you are reading this book means that you have thought about one thing, anyway: you would prefer to spend the rest of your life with a husband.

If so, you're in good company. Most divorced men and women do remarry, and they do it within six years of their divorce. (Widowed persons also remarry, but more slowly and in a smaller percentage.) Divorce doesn't necessarily mean that people reject marriage—only their choice of a

partner, and most believe that they can rectify that mistake
the next time around. More and more, divorcing is being
viewed as a step in one's personal growth, rather than as a
failure.

It really is OK to want to be securely mated. Though it
is certainly true that a woman can and should feel worthwhile without a man in her life, it is also true that many
women (and men!) find the single life alien to their person-
alities. They feel more comfortable and happier sharing
their lives with a partner.

Forget the myth that it is grim to be a divorcee or widow in today's society. It really can be an interesting, lively
time, and award you a Ph.D. in growth and change. This is
a great time for a woman to be single—there is no limit to
our horizons. I had *fun* as a single who was "pushing fifty,"
and so can any woman. It's primarily a matter of attitude.

It may be harder for a widow or for a woman whose
husband left her for another woman, say, to look upon single life the same way I did, because it was *my* decision to
leave my marriage. But after the initial shock wears off,
you, too, can look at your new life as having infinite possibilities to savor. You soon can be leading a full, and exciting
single life, but you will, however, have to do some concrete
things to help the process along. Behind any worthwhile
endeavor there is hard work. Too often, women expect
things to accrue to them without effort.

I *understand* that you live in many different circumstances. Some of you have young children at home, some
of you have teenagers living with you, some of you are now
completely alone in the world, some of you have money
problems, some of you have more education or natural
beauty than others—but *all* of you have the power to enhance yourselves and your lives. And the time to begin is
right now.

If you are recently divorced or widowed, you may be

afraid of the future. Don't be. You are probably exaggerat- *[lack of]*
ing in your mind how awful it is to be alone. For instance, *[touch ε]*
many of you still have your ex-husbands in the background *[reality]*
to help you with the child rearing, even if you have the primary custody. Some of these ex's are more involved than
others, but most will be some kind of help in an emergency.
You also still have friends and family. You may never have
balanced a checkbook, arranged your own vacation, or
handled plumbing or automobile problems yourself, but
trust me, these are all skills that can be learned easily. More
and more of you are involved in the business world these
days, and know how to manage both your own lives and
someone else's office or store. Even a woman who has "on- *[Good!]*
ly" managed a household and children has the executive
ability to run a small business! Think of the skills involved—the ability to handle several tasks at the same time
. . . to jump out of bed in the middle of the night and in-
stantly be alert enough to handle an emergency . . . to
tackle distasteful chores even when you're not in the mood
. . . to call on the great human-relations skills that have
smoothed out family relationships. You also have sexual
experience, maturity, and tenacity. Your sudden singlehood may be uncharted territory, but you entered that before when you married or started anything else new in your
life.

Yes, but I feel so alone.
Well, you aren't. You're in good company. Out of a total of
92,228,000 women in the United States, there are almost
twenty million unmarried women over the age of thirty
and almost fifteen million over the age of forty-five.
Among these, in the thirty-and-over age group, almost six
million are divorced and almost eleven million are widows.
Between 1960 and 1981, the number of divorcees in this
country grew by almost five million and the number of

widows by two and one-half million. Although the total
number of women in the country also grew by 16,300,000,
the fact remains that almost 27% of American women over
the age of twenty-nine are divorced or widowed.

That may be true, but I'm still hurting.
Depending on your stage of post-divorce or widowhood,
you may be suffering a variety of reactions, such as fear, anger, anxiety, guilt, depression, grief, or a loss of self-esteem. I can assure you that these feelings will all resolve
themselves over time. Eventually we all arrive at a stage of
acceptance and want to go on with our lives. The hurts will
continue to break through your consciousness from time to
time, but they need not cripple you emotionally nor prevent you from leading an exciting, spirited life. You may go
through an initial stage of frenzied dating and sex to reassure yourself that you are still attractive, or you may withdraw and mourn for a while, or you may isolate yourself
and dump all your energies into your work or your kids. So
be it. It is normal to manifest these extreme behaviors *in the
beginning*. But if they continue for longer than one year, I
think you should consider seeking professional help.

*Could you elaborate on this a bit? I don't know why
someone who isn't crazy would want to see a
mental-health counselor.*
First of all let's clarify this "crazy" business. The person
who can be helped the most through therapeutic intervention is the person who is *not* crazy, and who functions well
most of the time. He or she may be going through a period
of stress or may simply want to gain a better understanding
of the self. (I am excluding long-term, in-depth therapies
from this discussion. It is helpful to seek this type of treatment if you are beset by crippling anxiety, depression, severe neuroses, or a physical illness with psychic compo-

nents. A long-term psychoanalysis is also a method of re-
structuring your personality and the way that you handle
life, but few people have the time or the financial resources
for this.)

After the breakup of a marriage or a long-term relation-   ✗
ship, one goes through a period of mourning, whether or
not it is felt consciously. In addition, there is always a com-
ponent of anger or guilt. The one who leaves feels guilty
and the one who is left feels angry. If you don't deal with
these feelings, they can cause physical illness or depression
(remember, the body has a head). Some fortunate souls
have built-in mechanisms for dealing with stress in their
lives. They find relief in talking to close friends, through
meditation or relaxation techniques, or by ventilating their
feelings in other appropriate ways. Others of us need help
to recognize and vent our feelings. So, just as we might go
to a doctor for help in a physical crisis, we go to a qualified
mental-health professional during an emotional crisis.

In addition, those of us who have been divorced do not   ✗
want to make the same mistakes again. Without therapeutic intervention people often marry or become involved
with the same type of person over and over again in a self-
destructive cycle. In order to break out of that cycle, you
must gain self-understanding so that you can seek a more
fulfilling relationship the next time. A good therapist can
help you toward this goal. If you are a widow, it is important for you to deal with the mixed feelings created by your
loss (such as guilt, anger, fear of the future) and to mourn
adequately. You must do your "grief work" in order to resume a productive and happy life.

Group therapy is one helpful method of working
through these feelings. The group becomes a sort of extended family, and you learn about yourself by getting
feedback from the group and the therapist on how you relate to the other members. Since the group is a microcosm

of the outside world, you can transfer this new knowledge to your outside relationships. You can make some breakthroughs in old, neurotic patterns that may have prevented you from having as full a life as you wanted. The group also serves as an emotional support system when the world outside has been harsh. There you can get positive "strokes" when you need them, or straight talk when that is what you need.

No matter what type of help you choose, make sure you find a qualified therapist. Someone who is well recommended by your physician or by a person with first-hand experience is a good bet. Most communities have resources for those with low incomes, so don't let money problems discourage you from seeking help if you need it. A good place to begin your inquiries for low-cost help is with religiously based agencies such as Catholic Services, Protestant Family Services, or Jewish Family Services. Another referral source is your United Way agency. The credentials you should look for when choosing a therapist are clinical social worker with a master's degree in social work, psychologist with a Ph.D., psychiatrist with an M.D., or mental health counselor with a master's degree in counseling.

During and after a divorce, consider joining a divorce adjustment group. These groups usually go by the name of "Coping with Divorce" or something similar, and you can find them scattered among the adult-education courses given at your local high school, Y, junior college, or university. When I was leading these groups, I was struck by the universality of the pain caused by divorce, whether the marriage was of long or short duration, whether or not it involved children, or whether the couple was young or old. People just do not break up a marriage without suffering.

Are all divorcees losers?
Of course not. Sometimes we are just inexperienced, or un-

educated about how to choose a mate. We may have married for the wrong reasons, such as looks or romantic notions. Some people are just too young or immature to know what they need when they marry, and they're disappointed when they discover that their marriage doesn't fill their needs.

Here are three fairly typical examples of real women's failed marriages and their subsequent remarriages to more suitable partners:

"I was warned about Ray from the moment we were introduced. He was a singer and a musician, and the man who introduced us told my parents, 'Don't let your daughter get mixed up with this guy. He's no good.' Of course I proceeded to get involved with him, and for three years it was an on-again, off-again relationship. My parents and family knew he was wrong for me, but they tried not to interfere. I guess I had to get him out of my system because we finally did get married. We bought a home and things were all right for a while, but he was irresponsible and would lose jobs because he argued with his bosses. Meanwhile, when he did work, I sat home alone night after night because he was performing, and then I left for work early the next morning because I couldn't afford to quit my job. We hardly saw each other, and when we did see each other, we usually argued.

"After eleven months of this life, after I had become overweight and depressed, I left him. I was single for four years until I met a wonderful man, and we are now happily married. Sometimes it takes one marriage to bring home to us what we should look for in a husband."

"I was thirty when my husband left me. We had been college sweethearts and I had never really dated anyone else. He just left me and our two young sons after eleven years of marriage, and sent me a divorce notice through an attorney.

"I didn't know what I would do. I wasn't happy in our marriage, but I would have stuck it out because that's what people did in those days. Thank goodness I had parents who could help me. They supported me while I went back to school and got a graduate degree so that I could work. I dated a little, but with the two children, it wasn't easy. I was always worried about spending enough time with them.

"Meanwhile, through an introduction by friends, I met a man I really loved. After I met him it took three years for us to decide on marriage. He had to get used to the idea of marriage and children because he hadn't been married before. It was a lot for him to take on, and though we broke up a few times, we would always get together again. It was important for me to remarry. I missed the companionship and didn't enjoy single life that much. I was timid and shy, and it was hard for me to date.

"From the beginning of our dating relationship, John was not only concerned about me, but about the children as well. We've been married thirteen years now and have had a child together. My other children feel very close to John, and I now can even talk with their natural father without bitterness. He has also remarried and has children. Marriage is a much more comfortable life for me and I enjoy it. I realize now how unprepared I was for that first marriage."

"Morry and I were married twenty-four years when he came to me one day and announced that he was in love with someone else and wanted a divorce. I couldn't believe it. We had been childhood sweethearts, and inseparable since our marriage when he came back from the service after World War Two. We did without things for years while he went to college on the G.I. Bill, and we struggled to build up our business and raise the children. Then, when we should have been reaping the rewards of all this hard work and enjoying our life together, he hit me with this.

"I nearly had a nervous breakdown. I had to be medicated, and for weeks I didn't move out of the house—just lay around in bed crying. When I finally realized he wasn't going to change his mind, I tried to gather myself together, but it was a long time until I was able to face life again and feel like a worthwhile, whole woman. I couldn't think about ever trusting another man.

"But God was good to me and sent an old friend my way, who was also divorced. Jack didn't know that Morry and I weren't together anymore, and when he came to town he looked us up. When he called and I told him the sad story, he asked if he could come to visit me anyway. Over the course of several months we wrote to each other, and he visited several more times. We began to realize that we cared for each other, and tried to spend more and more time together. The happy ending is that we were married four years ago, and are ecstatically happy. I never thought I would enjoy life again as much as I am, and I have gained new strength and wisdom from the whole experience. If I survived, anyone can."

As you can see, it's easy to make a mistake the first time around or to end up without a husband as a victim of circumstance. None of these women were losers, as proven by their successful relationships with other men.

One anonymous writer wrote facetiously, "One's first husband must be suffered in much the same spirit as one's first pair of high heels . . . My advice, therefore, is to get the first marriage out of the way early in life, skipping the other phases and moving as quickly as possible from Honeymoon to Divorce. A good selection of husbands chosen carefully and changed frequently will keep your figure in

trim, your bank balance in good health, and most impor-
tantly your humour intact." As Dorothy Parker put it:

> Oh, gallant was the first love, and glittering and fine,
> The second love was water, in a clear white cup,
> The third love was his, and the fourth was mine,
> And after that, I always get them mixed up."

*Seriously, now, is there anything I can do besides going
for professional help that might keep me from making a
mistake the next time around?*
Yes. You can do some self-examination. Whether you're widowed or divorced, it's important to reexamine the dynam-
ics of your marriage and analyze what went wrong and
what was right about it. You don't want to duplicate destructive patterns in your future relationships, and you do
want to think about the kind of life you are seeking with a
new partner. Too often, women repeat their mistakes in
their selection of and expectations from men because they
are motivated by unconscious needs. Honest introspection
will help to overcome this. *Honesty* is the key word. Only
you can discover what makes you tick. This self-evaluation
is also important for widows, who tend to idealize their relationships with their dead husbands. Now is your chance
to take an honest look at your previous marriage without
the rose-colored glasses.

   To help guide you in your self-evaluation I have
devised a series of questions. If you do some hard thinking
along the lines that I suggest, you should be able to integrate your past life with your future needs and desires. Feel
free to write down your thoughts if you wish, but remember that the *thinking* is most important here. You should refer back to these questions often, because your answers
may change as new thoughts occur to you and as you gain
experience with men.

In the following section, the initials "F.H." will refer to your former husband and "P.N.P." to your potential new partner.

Here goes:

1. How did you and your F.H. express and demonstrate your love and caring for each other? Would you like it to be different in a new relationship? How would you like to change the way that *you* express these feelings?

2. What was your sex life like? How would you like it to be? The same? Different? How?

3. How open were you and your F.H. with each other? How did you settle differences? Do you want more or less openness with your P.N.P.? Are you comfortable with the expression of anger or negative feelings? If not, would you like to be?

4. How much personal space and freedom do you need and want? Was this a source of conflict in your previous relationship?

5. How did your children, if any, affect the relationship? How would you handle the relationship between the children, yourself, a new partner, and your ex?

6. Did his or your extended family cause problems? Would you handle them differently next time?

7. Were your F.H.'s personal habits acceptable to you? Did his mannerisms ever irritate or embarrass you? What is important to you in this regard?

8. Are health and fitness important to you in a P.N.P.? Did your F.H. take care of his body? Do you want your P.N.P. to be health- and fitness-

conscious? Do you want to improve your own
health and fitness? Does he have to enjoy the
same sports that you do?

9. Did your F.H.'s interests coincide with yours or
did they cause friction between you? Do you want
someone with many interests? Must they be the
same as yours?

10. Where does work fit into your life plan? Who do
you expect will assume the role of provider in any
future marriage?

11. Did the issue of money complicate your lives?
How did it relate to who had the power and control in your family? Would there be a better way to
handle finances in a future marriage?

12. What is your thinking about male/female roles?
Are you very traditional? Do you want to retain
the same type of roles in your future relationship
that you and your F.H. assumed?

13. What kind of life style do you want in the future?
Do you want more social life? Less? Do you want
to be affluent or the wife of a community leader?
Do you need to be part of a particular social class?

14. Which religious, social, and moral values do you
want your P.N.P. to share with you?

These questions should give you enough food for thought
to keep you ruminating for some time. They encompass all
the potential trouble spots that can rear their ugly heads in
a new marriage. Of course, there is always the possibility
that we will toss out all our ideas when we fall in love with
someone, so keep an open mind. Your thoughts about
these matters are not set in concrete—some flexibility is always a good thing.

What do most people look for in a second marriage?
Well, it certainly isn't perfection any longer. Most people
are looking for mutual caring, warmth, and friendship.
They put less emphasis on money and success, and they
have more realistic expectations about what marriage is
like. In general they have a more relaxed attitude toward
the whole matter. Formerly married people are usually
more self-aware, and they are not cynical about marriage,
even though theirs may have failed. Three-quarters of all
divorced men and two-thirds of all divorced women remarry. They feel that the next time can be different, and they
like the companionship and intimacy that marriage provides—but they also want the "right" person.

Marriage is a more natural way for most people to live,
and is good for health and longevity. Loneliness and/or the
single state are correlated with higher rates of illness, especially for men. Which brings me to another point. Marriage
is good for men, despite the bad press that they have given
it throughout the years. Married men have fewer illnesses
and live longer than single men. One tongue-in-cheek
Canadian, writing under the pseudonym "Putzi von Pince-
Nez," put it this way:

> Suddenly all the old rakes about town are getting married.
> How may one account for this amazing phenomenon? He
> quotes one such bon-vivant: "One day I woke up, had to get
> my own coffee, couldn't find a clean shirt, contemplated
> my dirty shoes, and thought to myself, 'enough is enough.'
> " Now married . . . he no longer concerns himself with
> these tiresome and unmanly chores. He awakes happily to
> his coffee and Globe brought to his bedside, chooses from
> an array of sparkling linen and admires his own contented
> reflection in his shining shoes. Alas, few men in these try-
> ing times can be bothered with the preliminaries neces-
> sary . . . for obtaining sex . . . so, we succumb. All of which
> goes to prove Oscar Wilde's aphorism that women marry
> because they are curious, and men because they are weary.

If we women can accept this statement without getting too angry, it can be an effective strategy for us in our husband search. <u>If you learn nothing else from this book, remember that men are looking for someone to take care of them!</u> More on that topic later.

Why do women remarry?
Following are some reasons given by the real-life women I interviewed:

> "I met a wonderful man. From the beginning of our relationship he was concerned not only about me, but about my children as well; we were a family. I was in love and felt that we had the potential for a good life together."

> "For financial security and companionship."

> "He gave me an ultimatum. Either I married him or it was over. I wasn't looking for remarriage, but I didn't want to lose him." (Several women gave this reason, much to my surprise.)

> "I couldn't muster up the energy for another affair. I just gritted my teeth and jumped in."

> "I wanted a child."

> "Loneliness, fear of the future alone, a belief that I had found someone to share my life."

> "I fell in love with my present husband."

People remarry for all kinds of other reasons, too. Some are looking for a father or mother for their existing or unborn children, or for a different life style. But most of them simply miss the good things about marriage, and after they begin to feel a new strength and independence, they want to share their lives with someone again.

Are widows different from divorcees?
Yes. For one thing, the remarriage rate for widows is lower than for the divorced. Many are not willing to think about getting involved with someone new, as they feel that nothing can compare with the marriage they lost. If they are interested in remarriage, however, how soon they do it depends largely on their age. They have the same problems with dating as divorcees do, but unlike most divorced women, they may have less interest in sex during the first year after their husband's death. Another difference is that the widow feels sadness rather than bitterness, although she may feel anger toward her dead husband for leaving her to cope with life alone. She is also free of the stigma of "failure" in marriage, and is accorded sympathy and comfort. A widow doesn't have to explain why her marriage didn't work, even if she knows secretly that it wasn't a good relationship. But, by and large, she is not ambivalent about marriage as an institution.

When a widow does remarry, however, she will often marry a widower, as they have an understanding that does not exist between the widowed and the divorced. Many widowed persons do not like the idea of an excess spouse floating around, who may turn up at inconvenient times. They have no frame of reference to give them a tolerance for these kinds of problems, so they usually seek out their counterpart when they look to remarry. But, a widow who wishes to remarry should follow the same guidelines that I have set forth for the divorced woman in her quest for a new mate—there are no differences between them when it comes to husband acquisition activities!

You mentioned possible competition with younger women for men. Do you have any hints about how I can have that competitive edge?
Yes. As I said in the introduction, this book is designed to

give you an edge that other women won't have. For now I will simply assure you that although you may be older, you have many things going for you. You have a history, a deeper knowledge of who you are, worldliness, glamour, maturity, and a mellowness that are very attractive to men. You know more about how to please men. You're willing to work harder to accomplish a goal because you've learned that there is no "free lunch" in life. You have usually nurtured at least one person, and you know that what you give to someone is not something that is taken away from you. You can project a warmth that is seductive. Surveys show that men love integrity, warmth, and friendliness in women, and you have plenty of those qualities. So remember that what you are looking for in a man is probably just what he is looking for in a woman.

What are my chances of remarrying despite the shortage of men?

Your chances are good. Women are marrying and remarrying every day. In 1980, one-third of all the marriages in the United States—some 1,209,467—were remarriages. Remember, contrary to popular belief, men *like* to be married. According to the prominent sociologist Jesse Bernard, once men have known marriage they almost can't live without it. And the famed social theorist Emile Durkheim stated that men need the constraints of marriage to keep from dashing themselves to pieces! Except for 1974 and 1975, the number of marriages has increased every year since 1958, and reached a new record in 1982. Also, the number of divorces declined in 1982 for the first time in twenty years.

The shortage of men exists only in certain age groups—after the age of thirty there *is* a surplus of single women. How did this come about? After all, men outnumbered women until about 1950. The most obvious reason is the wars, which killed off great numbers of the men that women over forty would now be marrying. Of the American men who would now be in their late fifties or early sixties, 292,000 died in battle in World War II plus an additional 113,842 from other causes and 34,000 in battle deaths in the Korean conflict plus 20,617 from other causes. In addition, although more male babies are born, more female infants survive the first year of life. Also, the mortality rates for the fifteen causes of death are all higher for males, and total life expectancy for men averages 7.5 years less than for women. Therefore, even a woman who remains married can expect to be alone in her late sixties or seventies.

Women born during the "baby boom" years of the late forties and early fifties who wish to marry men older than themselves have an additional problem, as no bumper crop of babies was born five or six years before the boom.

What do these figures mean in terms of finding another man to marry? They mean that you will have to change some of the patterns of thinking about living and loving that you still cling to, but which may no longer serve you in today's world. They mean that you may have to revise your ideas about who is eligible. (See Chapter Three for details.) They mean that you will have to start thinking more about how you can make the man you meet happy than about how he can make *you* happy! Don't get me wrong. You deserve happiness in love, too. But you'll considerably improve your chances of remarrying if you think of yourself as someone who will actively prepare yourself to find a compatible man. You may have to give up fairy-tale notions about waiting for a knight in shining armor to sweep you off your feet. Instead, with the help of this book, you can find someone to sweep off *his* feet! You'll find the quest lots of fun and very interesting, I promise!

How can I cope with my loneliness?
Right from the first, remember not to withdraw from your

old friends or your family. You mustn't make the mistake of living an entirely different life from when you were married. Although you may find that you are invited to parties less frequently as a solo, this condition is not so common as in the past. Many women who used to fear competition for their husbands no longer believe that all single women are predatory and prone to husband snatching. So, depending on your habits, your own attitude toward single guests when you were married, and the circles in which you traveled, you may still be included in some of your friends' social events.

But don't count on it. It will do you no good whatever to sit home hating your friends for excluding you or to go around complaining to anyone who will listen. What *will* help you is to understand that just because you are a single woman, you are not exempt from initiating or reciprocating hospitality.

This is how to create a whole pool of people who owe you invitations. Begin or continue to entertain. Give dinner parties. I invited each of my married-couple friends to dinner at least once, or if I didn't have the time or inclination to fuss, I took them to an elegant restaurant for Sunday brunch. Brunch in a restaurant is impressive at half the cost of dinner, which I couldn't afford. For dinner parties at home, I combined several couples at a time, sometimes including single female friends, daughters with or without dates, or whoever else I wanted to entertain at the same time. I tried to be sure that everyone was compatible, and always tried to include some good talkers in the group to keep things rolling. Sometimes I had a date for myself, but more often I didn't.

It wasn't long until I felt comfortable hostessing alone. Other women I know prefer to invite a man for themselves, and usually put him to work serving the drinks. But man or no man, no one ever refused my invitations, and they al-

ways seemed to have a good time. I encourage you to entertain as often as your funds and time allow!

Don't discourage yourself by lamenting that you don't
have the time or the cooking skill to entertain this way.
Even if you work full time, as I did, you can learn how to
whip up one or two quick menus or buy the food already
prepared from a specialty store. I usually started the dinner
two nights before the party. The first night I did the market-
ing, the second night I set the table and did any precooking
that was possible, such as fixing the dessert or cutting
things up, and the evening of the dinner I did the final
preparations.

You can also serve buffet style, so don't fall back on excuses about not having help to serve. I didn't. People really
appreciate an invitation to dinner, and it's a gracious custom. By the way, if you do have a special man in your life
when you entertain, it doesn't hurt for him to see what a
competent and charming hostess you can be. It might be
the catalyst for him to start thinking of you as *his* hostess,
forever.

Those people who never invited me back, I mentally
crossed off my list. I had an ongoing relationship with the
ones who did reciprocate, and we entertained back and
forth. Sometimes I was invited alone, sometimes I brought
the current man in my life, and occasionally they invited an
extra man for me. One sweet remarried lady, whom I had
known and befriended when *she* was single and *I* was married, often asked me over for week-night dinners with her
family. I learned to go to my friends' homes alone and to be
comfortable as an individual whom they enjoyed. It isn't
necessary to be half of a pair to be valued, but again, you
must remember that you aren't exempt from reciprocating.

Another very important point is that you must make a
deliberate, conscious effort never to arouse the slightest
suspicion that you are flirting with the hostess' husband or

current love. Don't allow yourself to get into a situation where the two of you are ensconced cozily alone in another room while she is busy in the kitchen. Try to be *visible*, and offer your help with serving and cleanup. Your women friends will not invite you back if they think you are flirtatious, even if they don't appear to notice at the time. This is *your* responsibility, no one else's.

Sometimes, no matter how hard you try, things can get awkward. One evening a former "steady" of mine and I invited a dear girlfriend of mine and her husband to dinner at his home. She came alone because her husband had a meeting, but he arranged to pick her up later. While I was fixing food, doing dishes, or cleaning up in the kitchen, the host (who I thought was in love with me) came on to her so strongly that it was all she could do to escape his advances. Every chance he got, he tried to corner her. It was embarrassing to both my friend and myself, and although our friendship survived, the love affair did not. In this case my friend was able to tell me how embarrassed and upset she felt, and it was clearly not her fault that he was lecherous. In other circumstances, however, *your* hostess might not be so understanding, and your loyalties not so strong. So, a word to the wise.

I must also stress the importance of women friends. They are fun and good to talk with, commiserate with, telephone, hang around with, and shop with, and a great consolation when you have man problems. You can both agree at least once a week that men "stink" and that you're swearing off them for the duration. I enjoyed and enjoy my women friends, and they were and are an important part of my life. I talk to them about my most intimate feelings, and they can understand in a way that men seem unable to. It's good to see that women are becoming less competitive about men and more committed to their friendships with one another.

What do you do if you have a date with a woman friend   ✕
and a man asks you out on a date for the same time?
This is the eternal question. The consensus seems to be that
if the man is "special" or if you have been trying to connect
with him for a long time, it is acceptable to ask your
girlfriend to excuse you this time. No woman *likes* it, however, when a woman friend cancels out on her. She may
have set time aside and looked forward to your plans. Unless there is sufficient notice, she can find herself adrift and
lonely that day. Though most will forgive an occasional
cancellation, no woman will continue a friendship with
someone who consistently dumps her in favor of a date.
The answer also depends on your philosophy about femi-
nism. Most feminists would consider such behavior unac-
ceptable, as it only reinforces the traditional view that
women are less important than men and that our endeavors are secondary to theirs. It's a tough issue to reconcile in
these times, when women outnumber men and you wish
to marry. It's always easier to be noble when you are only
theorizing and not being asked to make the actual sacrifice.
Circumstances never forced me to make this choice when I
was single, but I am sure that if a man called me for a date
and I was eager to know him, or had been hoping for a long
time that he would call, I would have asked my girlfriend to
be understanding and to let me off the hook. I would, however, also have given her the same consideration.

How else do people deal with their aloneness?
There are many time-honored ways to deal with being
alone, such as reading, hobbies, movies, plays, classes,
sports, and organization work, and they have been dealt
with in depth in many books and articles. They all stress
the difference between aloneness and loneliness. Loneliness has been described as a yearning for an attachment to
a person, while aloneness is merely the absence of other

humans. Sometimes aloneness is welcome—but loneliness, never. My worst days for loneliness were always Sundays, so I tried to plan something for that time. For others, Saturday night is bad. Be creative about solving this problem. Try to plan ahead for the times you know will be tough. I found that it wasn't hard to be alone on work days, but only when large periods of leisure time loomed before me. So I would invite guests over, visit a friend, plan an activity with my children—or do whatever I could think of to ward off the lonelies. Try to keep in mind that married folk feel lonely, too, especially unhappily married folk. Loneliness is painful while it lasts, but it will pass.

One formerly single lady I met often dined out by herself. She went to the same restaurants, and the staff grew to know her and would chat with her during dinner. She claims that she never felt self-conscious about dining alone even in the fanciest restaurants. *I* couldn't handle that. I would have dreaded the thought that I might run into some married people who knew me, or a former date with another woman, and that I might be looked upon with pity. But that was *my* hangup. This lady found that it made her life more interesting and gave her something to look forward to. She also traveled alone, as many women do, sometimes with tours, sometimes not. She found it enjoyable, and inevitably seemed to meet people. My husband, the former bachelor, traveled alone all over the globe for years while single, and he met women to eat with and spend time with. Therefore, women can also meet the single men.

If you're really interested in learning a sport or a new skill, do it to learn or enjoy the activity, not to meet men. The men may or may not come along as an ancillary benefit once you get involved in what you're doing. For instance, while I was trying to learn to play golf, there were always plenty of men around the driving range. Since I was usually involved in a relationship during that time I never tried to meet anyone, but now, while I go around the links with my husband, I see opportunities everywhere for meeting and getting to know men in a very comfortable manner. You're often paired up with someone or asked to join a twosome. Tennis, scuba diving, sailing, or whatever else interests you may also offer opportunities to meet men. But the big joke around our local ski club is that most women join only to meet men, not because they want to ski, and they are looked down upon. You don't want to be perceived that way. If you're genuinely interested in your sport, you can meet men *and* women as a fringe benefit, but your primary goals should be to keep fit and release your tensions.

Has anyone come up with new ideas about a solution to the man shortage?
Since it's not yet feasible to import men from another planet, some other extreme solutions have been suggested. One is permitting geriatric polygyny, wherein one man over the age of sixty marries two to five women in his age group. In this way they can pool their resources, and as they age, they will have more hands to care for the ill and to eliminate the loneliness and neglect that many elderly persons suffer. Other suggestions are the ménage-à-trois marriage, in which one man marries two women, and the multilateral or group marriage, in which three or more members commit to one another and are all married to one another. It would take a major change in society's attitudes for such unorthodox measures to be widely accepted.

One trend, however, is growing more and more apparent to *me*, although I have not read about it anywhere or seen it identified in formal sociological terms. I call it the "shared life plan for men." This refers to the many instances in which men are divorcing their wives after a marriage of considerable length, say, twenty years. By then, their children are usually grown and on the road to independence. The man then proceeds to marry another woman, maybe a younger one, and they may have children together and live together until his death while his former spouse goes on to another liaison, marriage, or a career. In this way *two* women have had the opportunity for a marriage of considerable duration, and for a home with a father present during their children's formative years. For approximately one-third of her adult life span each woman has shared a man's life and his procreative powers, and has enjoyed a married life.

This switching of marriage partners coincides neatly with the middle-aged identity crisis experienced by many men, when they fear the waning of their sexual powers and begin to question what their lives mean. Perhaps the women who are "abandoned" by these men could somehow cease thinking of themselves as victims, and see themselves instead as part of a social trend which has evolved out of necessity, which I predict will grow even stronger. As the pressure mounts from women who have not yet had the opportunity to marry or have a child, this arrangement may come to be an acceptable solution, and many men may be fathers, grandfathers, and stepfathers at the same time.

The number of older woman-younger man marriages will also increase because a disproportionate number of women in their forties and fifties may not find marriageable men in their age range. By some kind of divine retribution, the practice of older men marrying younger women will be duplicated by the wives they have cast off. Widows, too, will cease to look aghast at liaisons with much younger men. This change will require women to rethink traditional ideas; no doubt they will have to assume greater financial responsibility for the family, since many younger men are just starting their careers and their earnings will not peak until their forties.

Curiously enough, these trends will also solve many

ancillary problems for both sexes. Since a woman's sexual drive remains strong throughout her life, it is perfectly natural for her to have a potent sexual partner when she is older, while an older man may regain a feeling of youth with his younger partner. Of course, we women can also benefit from the feeling of youthfulness that a younger partner may engender. There may also be fewer widows as women cease to outlive their husbands.

I am not advocating any of these solutions, but merely identifying trends that I see. Many, many people are still meeting and marrying partners of their own age, including myself and my husband, who are in our fifties, and many of the women that I interviewed. It is important to some men and women to have a shared history with their mates and to come out of the same frame of reference. When I mention Artie Shaw, for example, my husband doesn't think he's the new comedian on *Saturday Night Live!*

Enough theory. It is time to move along now, to get started on the program that will help you find a man with whom to share the "five C's" of a good marriage: closeness, caring, companionship, comfort, and commitment.

CHAPTER TWO

The New You: Getting It All Together

Y ou're beginning to come to terms with your aloneness and learning to relish your new independence.
You know yourself better these days and are eager to live
your life to the fullest. You've decided that you want to remarry despite your bad experience or your loss. What next?

Your next step is to take the time for a complete self-ap-
praisal. Does your life or your image need sprucing up?
Now is the time for some enlightened selfishness and con-
centration on *you*. No matter how long you've been single,
it's helpful to stand back and take a look at yourself. You
want to be everything you can be in all areas of your life,
and this may entail spending more time on yourself than
you did when you were married. As you invest in your image, you will begin to like yourself better and better.

It can be very exciting to present your best self to the
world. Looks may not be everything, but they do count.
Why jeopardize your chances in love or work by refusing to
make the most of your appearance? Whether we like it or
not, there *is* a correlation between appearance and success,
so don't sabotage your chances for getting what you want
in life because of some old, stubborn idea that people have

to accept you "as you are or not at all." That attitude will get you nowhere. The "world" does not have time to dig beneath your dowdiness to discover the real you.

There are some things that you will just *have* to do. Your uniqueness and your strengths are not enough if the packaging is wrong. You've certainly heard the old joke about the guy who hit the mule over the head with a stick after claiming to be an expert in scientific animal handling. When asked why, he replied, "First you have to get their attention." Well, men aren't mules, but according to a poll in *Singles* by Jacqueline Simenauer and David Carroll, when a group of single men were asked what attracted them to a woman, looks were rated as very important by 29% of the men, 46% considered them somewhat important, 12% didn't care one way or the other, and 6% said they didn't matter at all. When questioned further, many agreed that looks counted only on first impression; after the first five minutes they were more interested in integrity, kindness, understanding, and a sense of humor. However, they still like women who are "neat, well-groomed, and who have a personal style." They find grossly overweight women and very heavy makeup a "turn-off," while graceful and happy looking women are a "turn-on."

The most consistently negative feedback I found in all my research was in the area of overweight. Not one man said that he liked fat women. Some of the dating services and marriage brokers I interviewed told me that they would not accept a client who was grossly overweight. Even most of the ads in the personal columns stipulate "slim female." No matter how much it hurts and angers us to be judged in such a superficial manner, this is the reality. You can hate it, fight it, rail against it, but despite the advances of the larger women who organize into groups, establish shops, and design clothes for the "big and beautiful" woman, there is a very pervasive prejudice in the United States against fat *people*, not just women. They are often discriminated against in the job market and perceived as losers. "Unfair," you say. "Yes," I reply—but we have to live in the real world and not in the land of make-believe. In the ideal world all people will be judged on their merits as human beings, but our present world is imperfect.

But I've been trying for years to lose weight—I don't know if I can.
This time your motivation may be greater. Do you remember how you planned for your education, your career, or a job interview? You put in a lot of time and effort. Well, part of your new "job" is to find a husband, and it is just as necessary to plan and work at this job as at any other. Most women who lose weight successfully state that it isn't important to conform to some unrealistic ideal represented on a chart or a magazine cover. If you lose enough weight to affect your self-image in a positive way, that's fine. We can't all be rail thin or conform to society's norms in any given era. At various times in history it was terribly chic to have a wasp waist, a flat chest, slim ankles, sloping shoulders, or a high forehead. I think that if you reach the point where you are pleased when you look in the mirror, look good in your clothes, and feel well, that's what it's all about.

So, let us begin. If you have decided that you should lose some weight after a really *honest* appraisal of yourself, there is only one way to get thinner despite the abundance of fads, theories, and el quicko diet plans. That is to eat fewer calories than your body uses for its work during a given time period. This work includes sustaining the vital functions of the body as measured by the basal metabolism rate, and your physical output. The suggested methods for accomplishing this goal are legion. If laid end to end, the number of diet books, diet clubs, and diet programs would cover an enormous distance. Make an informed decision and find a safe program that works for you.

I wouldn't dare incur the wrath of these people by rec-
ommending any one program except for Overeaters Anonymous, which is a wonderful support group for compulsive overeaters. I will, however, tell you a few things you
should know. Our bodies betray us in several ways. As
women, we have a thicker layer of fat than men, and it is
more difficult for us to reduce. Also, as we decrease our
food intake, the body slows down its metabolism as a
throwback to ancient times of starvation or food deprivation, thereby slowing down the rate at which we lose
weight. As a result of all these disgusting facts, we have a
heck of a time losing weight. It's hard enough before menopause and worse after menopause, but don't give up. It can
be done. Thousands and thousands of formerly fat women
are now slim.

*If you won't recommend a diet, at least tell me how I
can be more successful this time with my dieting.*
The only solution for getting thinner and staying that way
is to alter your lifestyle from this day forward. This means a
permanent way of eating that's different from the one that
made you overweight in the first place, not just a diet that
will last two weeks or a month. I have gleaned all the information available on all the safe ways to lose weight and
maintain the loss, and the best regime for both health and
weight reduction appears to be one that greatly resembles
the diet of our Asian neighbors. The following eating rules
will slim you down and keep you that way and should enhance your health. Be sure to check with your doctor before
making any drastic changes in your diet, since you may
have a condition that precludes eating in this manner.

1. Eliminate as many fats as possible from your diet.
   Since we still need calcium, drink skim milk and
   eat only skim-milk cheeses, while cutting down

on butter, shortenings, oils, margarines, and fatty meats. Another reason to eliminate most fats from your diet is that fats are being implicated in the development of cancer of the colon, breast, and possibly the endometrium (the lining of the uterus). Saturated fats are also implicated in the development of atherosclerosis.

2. Cut down on salt or eliminate as much of it as possible. Don't wait until you get high blood pressure to do so. Educate yourself about the foods that are high in salt and *sodium,* also, and be aware that canned and frozen foods and baked goods can be very high in content. Pickles, pickled meats, olives, cured meats, and anchovies are also big offenders.

3. Eliminate sugar from your diet. We can all live without it.

4. Increase your intake of complex carbohydrates, such as fruits, vegetables, and grains. Steam them or eat them raw. All vegetables are OK to eat, even sweet and white potatoes and rice, as long as you don't eat them with butter or sour cream. Eat more vegetables of the cabbage family, such as broccoli, brussels sprouts, cabbage, and cauliflower. The latest research shows that they are a preventive measure against cancer of the colon. These foods will also increase the amount of fiber in your diet which will help to prevent constipation and provide better nutrition.

5. Eat chicken (with the skin removed) and fish, instead of red meat and pork. Try to use them as the Asians do, in small amounts to season a dish instead of as a complete course.

6. Drink the purest water you can find, and lots of it. Try not to drink sodas that are sugared or artificially sweetened. Instead, use mineral waters and seltzers with a slice of lemon.

7. Limit your intake of alcohol to one drink a day or eliminate it entirely until you reach your weight goal.

8. Eat lower on the food chain. Instead of eating the animal or bird that consumes the grains, fruits, or vegetables, eat the grains, fruits, or vegetables yourself.

9. Eliminate caffeine from your life, but do it gradually, as it is a powerful drug and you can get a severe reaction to sudden withdrawal. I once experienced this on a weekend trip to a health resort, where I got deathly ill with diarrhea, vomiting, and a headache so severe I wanted to die. Only later did I learn it was because no coffee was served there, and I had experienced withdrawal symptoms.

10. Use artificial sweeteners only in moderation, as the jury is still out on their safety.

If you change your diet to follow these rules, you should lose weight, be more energetic, and stay that way forever. It will happen gradually over time without your ever counting one calorie! You must learn to like a lighter cuisine, and brainwash yourself that you no longer like the heavy, fatty foods that push up the scales.

As an aside, I greatly reduced the sweats associated with menopause by taking vitamins A, E, B complex, and C. It's worth a try if you are experiencing these symptoms, but be sure not to overdose on E or A, as they can build up in the body and cause toxic reactions. Ask an expert about the safest dosages for you.

WORK THAT BODY

Just when you thought you were safe, here comes the part about exercise. I know you're tired of hearing about its benefits, but unfortunately everything you hear is true! Exercise helps reduce stress and alleviate depression, improves your posture, lifts your behind, increases the rate at which you burn calories even up to four hours after stopping, firms you up to the point where you no longer jiggle and can throw away your girdle forever, and—believe it or not—has been shown to reduce appetite. It's unrealistic to think we'll look as good as Jane Fonda or Victoria Principal if we exercise, but we will certainly have *our* best possible body, and that's a worthwhile goal!

There are two kinds of exercise—aerobic and muscle toning. You should do some of each. Aerobics increases the efficiency of your respiratory and circulatory system and burns up plenty of calories, and muscle toning exercise will firm and shape you. Try to do something you like, so it won't seem tedious. For aerobics you can try running, jogging, fast walking, bicycling, swimming, jumping rope, singles tennis, racquetball, skating, or aerobic dancing. For muscle toning you can lift weights, use machines such as the Universal or Nautilus, or do yoga or calisthenics. See your doctor before undertaking a new exercise program!

That's fine if you're a jock, but I'm the world's worst athlete!
So am I, but here's how I kept healthy, slim, and fit when I was single. I went to a gym after work about three times a week, did an exercise routine with Nautilus and free weights, and took a whirlpool, steam bath, or sauna. This

routine was very relaxing after a day at the office, kept me from overeating, and helped me to sleep better. Almost every morning, I walked and jogged one mile outdoors. I had to get up at 6:30 a.m. to do it because I had to be in the office by 8:30, but it was worth it. I looked and felt so great afterward that I started the day with a real bang! If you don't live in a warm climate and can't get outdoors, you can use a stationary bike or a jump rope, or do some aerobics to music or a video before starting your day's activities. If you can possibly afford it and can spare the time, I suggest that you join a gym, preferably a co-ed facility. Co-ed gyms are not only a good place to meet men in an informal way, but knowing that the guys are going to see you in your leotard is an added incentive to work out. If you're not comfortable with the idea of a co-ed facility, that's OK, too. The important thing is that you exercise! If money is a problem, the community centers or YWCAs are usually affordable, and most public schools have programs as well.

Do you have any other tips for shaping up?
Yes. I rarely went out to dinner unless I was invited or it was a date. It wasn't only that I wanted to economize, but it's easier to watch your diet when you eat at home. Also, I'm hypoglycemic and I get ravenous at lunchtime, so I always eat big lunches. I tried to eat at cafeterias, fish restaurants, or salad bars, where I could eat large quantities of nonfattening foods like chicken, fish, vegetables, and salad. At home, I ate either steamed veggies, broiled chicken without the skin, or just an apple if I wasn't hungry.

Try eating more at lunch and less at dinner. You accomplish several things this way: you stand a better chance of using up the calories before going to sleep; you have digested your food before going to the gym after work but still have energy for exercising, and you don't have to stock your refrigerator with lots of fattening foods.

Here are some tips for when you have a dinner date. If
you have a last-minute invitation to dinner and have already eaten your big lunch, order only a shrimp cocktail or
a small salad plus a glass of wine. No man really minds this,
as it saves him money, and as long as you are chewing at
the same time he is, he won't feel uncomfortable. You can
also order only the vegetables that usually come with dinner, such as a baked potato (no butter) and a broiled tomato, or whatever they are serving that night (never turn
down a date just because you've already eaten!). If I knew
in advance that I was going out, I cut down on my lunch calories to make up for the larger dinner I knew I would eat.
Most men get upset with women who order a big dinner
and only eat a few bites, and I don't blame them. So use
common sense about how you order. You can't store up
food except as fat on your body, and you don't want *that!*

assumption: the man always pays [handwritten margin note]

What do I do about food for my kids?

If you have children, you should think of keeping foods in
the house that give you and them better nutrition per calorie, instead of just empty calories. Kids really don't *need*
chocolate, cookies, sodas, and ice cream. But, they can
have it for their school lunch if they must, or buy it after
school on the way home. At home they can snack on pop-
corn (without butter, this is a very low-calorie and healthful
snack), juices, fruit, whole-grain muffins, raisins, and
nuts. Many of our young generation are even embracing
the vegetarian style of eating. Pasta is a good choice, too. It
isn't fattening if you stay away from sauces that use
cheeses, butter, oils, and meats. It's also healthy and kids
love it. You can make all kinds of delicious dishes with all
kinds of pastas and never get bored. Try whole wheat, tomato, and spinach noodles for variety, with tomato and
vegetable sauces. Asian grocery stores are good sources of
fantastic noodles for stir-fries and other kinds of dishes.

Learn how to use tofu, a high-protein, low-calorie food made from soybeans. Adolescents in particular, even the boys, like to cook and experiment with exotic foods, so give them free rein in the kitchen to develop their skills. Your college kids will also come home with all kinds of cooking ideas, and you can learn a lot from them.

What happens if I'm very involved with a man and busy with my job, my house, and my children? How can I make time for all this?
HERE IS AN ABSOLUTE RULE!!! No matter what else is going on in your life, set aside time for your body and your health. The men in our lives come and go, but our bodies are forever! There is a tremendous difference between the look of an exercised body and an unexercised one, especially in women of a "certain age." Also, we can't afford to be sick. There is no husband around to nurse us, and medical care is expensive. So eat in a healthy manner, don't abuse alcohol or drugs, and take some vitamins even if you're running about in a frantic manner and working long hours. Read up further on good nutrition and exercise. All the things your mother told you are true. If you eat your vegetables you really will be healthy, and for those of you with children, you'll be setting a good example. Cooking the right foods takes no longer than frying a hamburger, especially if you invest in a microwave oven. Your veggies can be done in eight minutes; even a baked potato cooks in only ten minutes.

FACE UP!

Now that you're on the road to slimness and good health, perhaps your makeup needs a boost. Some kind of skin-care and makeup regime is an absolute necessity. The natural look is beautiful, but the natural look does not mean no makeup. Every woman needs a little bloom on the rose after she passes her teens. A minimum makeup consists of a moisturizer or sheer foundation for skin protection, some form of blusher or rouge, a lipstick or gloss, and mascara if your lashes are light. For daytime, it's best to stick to a natural palette of colors such as earth tones for eyes, brown mascara, peach blushers, and coral or clear red lipsticks. For evening, go a little crazy and experiment with heavier glosses, darker blushers, and glamorous eye makeup.

The best thing you can do is read, read, read about makeup, and experiment. The next best thing you can do is blend your makeup like mad! After it's on, wipe off some of your rouge or blusher and take a very critical look at yourself to see what more should go on and what can come off. Always use a magnifying mirror when applying your makeup. It's scary to see all those pores and lines, but you'll do a better job. If it looks OK magnified, it's sure to look OK to the naked eye. You don't have to buy expensive cosmetics, either. All the experts agree that there is very little difference between the most expensive and least expensive kinds. Beauty-supply stores are fun to shop in and they always have samples to try.

Do you think I should pay an expert to make my face over?

The average woman doesn't have access to the really good makeup artists, and usually has to depend on the department-store makeup consultant, who is pushing her products, or the women who also give facials. These people inevitably overdo it and you end up looking garish and theatrical. Most makeup artists also tend to push camera techniques, and their makeup is usually too heavy, too daring, and too artificial for the everyday world. They use too heavy a base, too dark a lipstick, and too extreme an eye makeup for most women to wear to work or even on a date.

A good rule is that the younger you are, the more extreme your makeup can be. Older women look harsh and ridiculous in the far-out looks that you see in fashion magazines; don't let anyone tell you otherwise.

Take good care of your skin and do it faithfully. Dermatologists agree that the sun is your skin's worst enemy. If you must sunbathe despite the damage it does to skin, be sure you use some form of sun protection. The sunblocks are numbered according to strength, ranging from moderate protection to #15, which is a complete sun block.

HAIR

A flattering, contemporary hair style is one of the most important components of your image, whether you like it short, long, straight, or curly. Try your best to find a look you can care for yourself.

Your best investment is a truly great haircut! Keep trying until you find that genius with the scissors who knows how to get the best out of your hair. You don't have a lot of time for hairdresser appointments, and you never know when you'll have a last-minute date. Find that style you can wash and fix yourself with hot rollers, a curling iron, or a blow-out. And wash your hair often. Sweet-smelling, silky, swirly hair drives men wild. Unfortunately I never had silky, swirly hair, but take heart, I found a husband anyway! I have coarse hair that bristles at the sight of a raindrop or humidity, and gets terminal frizzies. And to make it worse, I live in the most humid climate possible. A good haircut is even more important to people with hair like mine, but anyone's hair can be kept clean and under control with a little effort. So, no excuses. Spend whatever it takes to get a terrific haircut, because you need one only about every six weeks. If you spread the cost out over that time period, expensive doesn't look so bad.

*Do you think I should color my hair? I've heard that
men like blondes.*
There's no hard-and-fast rule about whether to color your
hair. I do. Gray can be gorgeous, but you might want to experiment with color to see if it adds or detracts from your
appearance. You can use temporary colors, try on differ-
ent-colored wigs, or go to an expert for advice. If you do
color your hair, gray or not, be sure your roots are *always*
done. The price of beauty is eternal vigilance! The day your
roots are showing will be just the day you run into that terrific man you've been dying to impress. Not that he will
necessarily notice, but *YOU'LL KNOW* and it will undermine your self-confidence. Anything that undermines
your self-confidence will telegraph to others and since we
need all the confidence we can get, don't dissipate it need-
lessly on things like —horrors—"root neglect."

What about excess hair?
I think eyebrows and moustaches belong in this section.
Unless you look like Brooke Shields, eyebrows need to be
plucked (in moderation—stray hairs only). Any superflu-
ous hair on your body should be shaved, waxed, or electro-
lyzed away, especially upper-lip and chin hairs. I have un-
dergone hundreds of hours of electrolysis, but they pay off.
Shave your legs and your armpits. Only Italian movie stars
can get away with not shaving, and even most of them
shave now. Nothing is uglier than little hairs poking out of
your stockings or long ones hanging from your armpits as
you raise your arm to caress his hair—in our culture it just
doesn't play. If you want to go against the norm you must
accept the fact that you may repel some men.

PLASTIC SURGERY

Whether or not to undergo surgery is a very personal decision. Don't listen to what others say. If you feel that you

would like to do something with your face or body, consult at least two plastic surgeons. If they both feel that surgery will help you look fresher, more beautiful, or smoother—*then* you can decide whether to go ahead and lift, peel, or chisel away the parts of you that are not pleasing to your eye. I know many women who have had beautiful results from facelifts and peelings, and even more who have benefited from breast lifts or nose reshapings. I feel that it helped some of them to remarry, as it greatly enhanced their appearance and motivated them to change other aspects of their looks and their lives to match the parts that were altered. Anything that makes you happier or gives you greater confidence has my full support and blessing, and will, no doubt, be supported by your loved ones. CAUTION: Find the best plastic surgeon in town. This is no time to shop for bargains.

CLOTHES

Clothes have to be a large item in proportion to your budget. When you're single it's important to look good whenever you leave the house because you never know when you will run into someone you haven't seen in a while, what man will pop up (I even met someone through an encounter in my building elevator), or when you may be invited somewhere while at the supermarket or dry cleaner. You also have to look sharp at work. Even if you wear a uniform, you can still express yourself in your accessories.

I don't have a lot of money. Is it possible to look great without spending a lot?
Looking well dressed on a small budget will tax all your creative resources and can be a great challenge. There are many money-saving tricks, such as shopping at the discount stores and outlet shops and taking advantage of

those never-ending sales to fill in your wardrobe. Take a good look at your present wardrobe and throw out all the old polyester knits that may still be hanging around. If you have a friend who is particularly talented at putting clothes together, ask her to come over and go over your wardrobe with you to figure out how to get the most mileage out of what you already own and help you decide what you need to buy to fill in the gaps. In addition, plenty of women swear by the thrift stores and used-clothing shops. I have tried shopping them without success, but some women have enough style and imagination to choose these clothes, add or subtract just the right touch, and wear them with great flair. If you can do this, you will save a lot of money and no one will be the wiser.

Buy classic clothes, not faddy things; they're a better investment. Besides, I discovered that men like a classic, classy, subtly sexy look, such as a tailored silk or silk-looking shirt, open just low enough to create some interest without showing too much cleavage, and a well-fitting skirt with a subtle slit. Add a few pieces of good-looking jewelry (it can be fake), a belt, some beautifully cut pumps or sling-backs, and you can go just about anywhere except a black-tie dinner or a fancy party. Men may stare at women in clinging, plunging, see-through, dangling, and feathered clothes, but they would be embarrassed for "their girl" to dress like that. Most men don't want other men to think that their woman is cheap or promiscuous, and at some level, they would really like her to wear Peter Pan collars and oxfords if they could talk her into it.

When I was invited on a trip, or to something really special that necessitated wearing clothes I knew I would never use again, I would try to borrow something. My friend Marilyn had some great jewelry and clothes that I would dip into for special times. Most of you have a "Marilyn" somewhere to borrow from.

Other basics that you will need are jackets, coats, sweaters, T-shirts, jeans and slacks. Buy the best you can afford. Sales are terrific for filling in and for the few faddy things you can't live without. Usually you can buy high fashion and regular hosiery, bathing suits, beach coverups, belts, leotards, tights, sweatsuits, hair ornaments, scarves, lingerie, purses, hats (which men love), gloves, and such at sales. You can accumulate a collection of these things over the years, as they are usually ageless in style.

Are there any special clothes I need now more than before?

Yes, as a single gal interested in husband acquisition, you will need a stock of robes and long flowing goodies to wear "at home." They look great for serving breakfast if your man spends the night, and they're elegant for at-home evenings and dinners "à deux." The less you wear under them the better, because you can show your curves without giving up your ladylike look; however, they should be opaque enough to leave something to the imagination. I find that I move differently in a long dress, and there is something about a woman in a long, flowing graceful garment that is very provocative to men. Remember, though, these clothes are for "at home" only. You'll look out of place anywhere else in a flowing caftan unless it is a beach robe made for that purpose, or an obvious evening gown worn to a formal affair.

Is that all I need to know about dressing?

A quick word about lingerie. You need pretty lingerie now more than ever. Throw out all the old serviceable briefs and bras that are made like iron maidens. Wear low-cut panties if you don't look good in bikinis, and softer, unstructured bras. Some women give up panties altogether and just wear panty hose. (Be sure they have cotton crotches to prevent vaginal fungi.) The new one-piece "teddies" are stunning if you have the body for them, and the garter-belt-and-stocking revival is a sexy option for women who can carry it off (it requires firm thighs). We all know that we wear different lingerie when we go out on a date that may end up in bed, but we can also wear pretty lingerie under our business clothes—it makes a woman feel differently about herself when she knows she's wearing something beautiful next to her skin.

You younger women who can go braless will, of course, continue to do so. But be sure to wear a bra when you do your jogging or aerobic dancing, as the tissue in your breasts can break down from the jiggling, and you may sag.

Some general rules about clothes are to buy the best you can afford and to make sure your clothes are always pressed. Sometimes I would be pressing something on the floor of my bedroom while my date waited in the living room, but if I hadn't had time to do it before, I did it then. Also, make sure your clothes are always clean and not torn. Examine everything when you take it off and sew what's torn immediately. Put whatever is soiled into the laundry or take it to the dry cleaner as soon as possible. There's nothing worse than needing something only to find that it's unwearable. In our busy, spontaneous lives we don't need surprises in our closets.

GROOMING

Clean is beautiful! This is not the time in your life to be careless about grooming. Remember your daily shower or bath; twice a day is better, and *always* before a date. After bathing use underarm deodorant and a lotion on your body to keep your skin seductively soft. You can't expect to have a sexily soft, smooth-skinned body if you only moisturize it before

a date. It must be done daily. Live your life like a girl
scout—always prepared.

Your nails should always be clean, too. If you wear nail
polish, keep it fresh and don't let it get chipped. I can't keep
my polish unchipped, so I wear colorless polish. Men really
do notice these things.

Use scent every time you dress—lighter colognes for
work, and a more intense perfume for evening. Try to carry
a clean, fresh handkerchief; with lace, if possible. Keep
your shoes polished and repaired. Run-down or scuffed
heels make you look down and out. And try to keep your
purse neat. This is a losing proposition for me, but I do try.
A sloppy purse can turn some men off.

POSTURE

Well—I feel a little like Pygmalion. We now have you slim,
healthy, gorgeously made up, dressed, and groomed.
DON'T RUIN IT ALL BY WALKING AS IF YOUR BODY IS
A BUNDLE OF RAGS! Stand up straight, walk with energy
and grace, and try to glide instead of bounce. All beautiful
women have good posture. Think about it. And all sexy
women walk beautifully and slowly. Can you picture Joan
Collins hurrying? Also be conscious of how you use your
hands. Men go wild over the graceful Asian woman who
has learned from birth to use her body and her hands gracefully. Once, when I was simply stirring coffee in a styro-
foam cup, a guy told me, "You do that so *well*." I never forgot it!

Whew! Do you get the feeling that you'll be spending
90% of your life on personal upkeep? Take heart. Once all
this becomes routine, it consumes only a small portion of
your time. Other than the hours spent in exercise and shopping, the other things are a matter of minutes. You can
learn to do a full makeup in about seven minutes, and once

your clothes are organized, upkeep becomes simple.

Now let's wind up your program with a discussion of your health, your home, your money, and your job, all important factors in your life as a solo lady.

YOUR HEALTH

Your health care is more important now than ever. You may or may not be aware of the stress scales formulated by our friends, the psychologists. They have assigned numerical ratings to various life situations. When you accumulate a certain number you are susceptible to illness. Divorce and death of a spouse are way up there in number of points. Combine that with other stresses, such as a change of residence or a job change, and you are very vulnerable.

You can combat stress in many ways. For me the best way is to work it out through physical exercise. There is strong evidence that exercise affects emotional well-being by releasing natural tranquilizing substances in the brain. Others may prefer meditation, going to church or synagogue, taking time out for beloved hobbies, or taking a nap. Find your favorite stress beaters and take the time to use them.

The exception to this is using alcohol. It's not only unhealthy, as I mentioned earlier, but drinking to relax is a bad habit because you can become psychologically or physically addicted. Besides, the sedative effect is only temporary. Alcohol has a kickback effect of irritating the nervous system after several hours, therefore defeating the original purpose of relaxation.

As I've said, you can't afford to be ill now that you have no husband to take care of you and you have to work. Illness is also expensive, and most of you must make do on less money. Fortunately, I was only sick twice—with colds—in my three years of single life. I had one scare with a breast lump that turned out to be a cyst, thank goodness. That was discovered during a routine physical examination, which brings me to another aspect of your health: regular examinations. See your gynecologist at least once a year, or twice if possible. Have annual physical and dental exams without fail. My dear sister died at age fifty-three from cancer of the colon. It might have been detected earlier if she had had a rectal exam, but she hadn't had one since the birth of her last child some twenty years before. So please, even if you hate going to the doctor and dentist as much as I do, go anyway! If you take care of your teeth and your body, they will serve you well. They're the only ones we have, so we really have to cherish them until our final days (which we do not have to rush into; they come soon enough).

HOME SWEET HOME

Where you live is important. Early in my singlehood, I was advised not to move way out to the boondocks, or no man would date me. I would be "G.U."—geographically undesirable. So I did not buy a delightful townhouse, and I moved to a more central location at the same price. The irony is that my first three men all lived in the area I had rejected. I think there's a lesson to be learned here. Live in an environment that's pleasing to *you*. I know at least two women who were courted by men who lived at the other end of the *country*—love will find a way!

Of course, some of you may not have a choice of where you live. You may have to stay in the home that you shared with your husband because of finances or your children's needs. It's hard for kids to have to move away from their friends and neighborhood, and they've had enough upheaval in their lives from the change in the familial situation. If you rent, it's difficult to find places that accept children. So, within your budget and other limitations, try to live in the very best quarters you can. This is not the place to scrimp. If you must, scrimp on car, clothes, or food (you can eat very healthfully for little money if you cut down on meat), but not on your home. It's important to have the soul satisfaction of living in the nicest possible environment. You need a haven after making a living all day, and a place of peace and repose to enjoy with your children and your friends. In addition, men tend to spend a lot of time at their lady's home, and your home is also part of the ambience that you project when a date picks you up.

So try to create the most restful and lovely setting that you can within your limitations. Your old home may need a facelift and a little sprucing up. No clutter, please, and lots of openness. Keep your colors neutral, with just a few bright accents and plants. Have some nice glasses, dishes, and linens for entertaining. Let men see what they have to lose if they let you slip through their fingers. Men, especially mature men, love comfort, and they are always looking for mothering. So create a place where it's easy to be nurturing, with a nice comfortable easy chair where he can put his feet up. Have some liquor and wine around to offer your dates. Men appreciate thoughtfulness as much as women do.

MONEY, MONEY, MONEY

Another problem is money: how to manage it, and—a big bugaboo for most of us—how to acquire it! Unfortunately, dating doesn't help the single woman much with her everyday expenses. Men think that the single woman has it "made" because they usually take her out to dinner, buy the theater tickets, and so forth. In my experience, however, this is not the stuff on which single women spend their money. Even if you don't have children to support, dating won't cover any important expenses. The entertainment and the gifts you receive from men are icing on the cake of your life, but the major portion of your income will go for mundane things like car expenses, medical expenses, clothing, rent, food, and mortgage. Travel, dinners out, and costly cultural events simply are not within the average woman's budget. It's very important not to overextend yourself.

Everyone has a different income and different expenses. I found that I could cut corners by shopping wisely for food, by driving a reliable, economical car, by trying to stay healthy, and by not indulging in expensive restaurant dinners. My major expenses were clothes, mortgage, insurance, and utilities. Make a realistic assessment of your assets and income. You can always find ways to manage money better, even if your income is not great. Educate yourself about financial planning and how to save dollars on your income tax. Being a woman is no longer an excuse for being ignorant about money. Many of you may find yourself in possession of a lump sum of money for the first time in your life because of a divorce or death settlement, and it's easy to let this money slip through your fingers if you don't plan seriously. It can dissipate in small amounts for things that have no permanent value. I invested most of my share from the sale of my former home in a condominium apartment for myself and in a deposit on another apartment, preconstruction, which I planned to resell for profit. I did this for two reasons. First, I wanted the deduction that the mortgage interest provided for my income taxes. Second, I wanted the security of a roof over my head and an investment that would retain its value or appreciate if I had to liquidate it. This decision proved to be wise, because when I remarried, I sold my apartment for quite a bit more than I had paid for it. The investment condo never materialized, however; my deposit was returned along with the interest it had accrued while in escrow for two years, so nothing was lost.

Investigate thoroughly before you invest. Many a widow or divorcee has been bilked out of her money by smooth-talking salesmen and bad investments. Stocks are very risky, and you should only invest in them with money you can afford to lose. Investments in gold and other commodities can be losers, too, if you don't know what you're doing. Never invest in a business as a minority stockholder unless you are fully aware that you have no power or say-so in the business. You can regain your money only if there is an agreement that you'll receive a share of the profits, if you sell your share to someone else, or if the business is sold. Have a good lawyer look over any documents before you sign them. Later, I'll go into detail about avoiding "gold-digging" men who may be after your assets.

What else?
It was really tough for me to get credit when I was first divorced, and it probably still is a problem for a woman whose credit was always in her husband's name. The same can be said for car insurance. I was refused coverage by the company that covered me while I was married, so I had to track down and establish my own providers of credit and insurance. It took a long time for me to get my first credit card, but once I got one, the others came along easily. I found an insurance company to cover my car with some effort. My job provided me with hospital insurance, a very important aspect of security. If you don't work, you may find it expensive and difficult to get coverage.

Avoid overextending yourself on your credit cards—you can really get into a bind. One good piece of advice (from an expert in consumer credit) is not to use cards to charge restaurant meals. By paying cash in restaurants, you are less inclined to spend extravagantly and you won't be stuck with big bills long after the memory of the meal is gone. Use your credit cards mostly for large purchases, or for times when you might be in a cash-flow squeeze, such as Christmas, outfitting the kids for school, or emergency travel. Read some good consumer guides to plastic spending, because it's no fun to have money problems.

This is a good time to discuss your job, because none of these suggestions will help if your income isn't great enough to cover even the bare essentials. "*What* job?" you may ask. I'm talking about the one you are going to get if you don't already have one. <u>Yes, you should work even if you don't need the money, which is rare these days</u>. Don't stay home or spend your time doing only volunteer work. A job takes you out of the house and into the world, makes you a more interesting person, and helps you meet people. It also helps you through the hard times. When I thought my world was collapsing around my ears, I *had* to get up and go to the office. There were people there who liked me, and even though I didn't tell them my problems (a good policy), I could eat with, talk to, and work with human beings who valued me. Bless my jobs. They saved my soul many a day. They also kept me eating and gave me a sense of increased self-esteem and competence, and they can do the same for you. There is nothing quite like the "high" you feel from a job well done. Men have been grooving on it for years!

But I've always been a housewife! Who would hire me?
If you have never worked, try to determine what skills you already possess that could transfer to full-time employment. Read vocational information and contact the agencies that specialize in getting the displaced homemaker back to work. Vocational counseling is usually available in large cities for little or no cost. Your YWCA is a good place to begin your inquiries. You will have to work up a resume,

which you can do with the help of books to be found in your library. <u>Your first job may not be the ideal one that you wanted, but it can be the first step on a career ladder.</u> I had a heck of a time getting my first job after being out of circulation for nineteen years, but a lady boss finally took a chance and hired me. After the first job, the others come more easily because you can show some recent experience on your resume. Try to find a first job that will prepare you for a next step, and if you plan carefully, it can set off a chain reaction that might lead to a career.

   <u>Your goal at all times is to earn enough to live the lifestyle you want until the right guy comes along, and *after*.</u> Never be afraid to take a clerical or secretarial job; business is quicker these days to recognize ability, and you can rise in the hierarchy. Government jobs offer good entry-level positions, and examinations are often the basis for hiring, so if you pass with a decent score you have a good chance. Look into your county, city, state, and federal government for job announcements and openings. I took all the tests, and some were quite easy. Also try the large public utilities, such as the electric or phone company. Most of them are committed to placing more women in nontraditional jobs, and if you're interested in what was formerly considered a "man's job," such as telephone lineman, you may have an even better chance. These employers are also committed to a policy of promoting from within the company, so your opportunities are virtually unlimited once you are *in*. That is why I emphasize that you can take an entry-level position at first, to insure that you will be in the right place when openings become available at higher levels.

   If you have little or no higher education or training, you may want to go back to school for some classes. Affordable classes are given now at all times, even weekends, and anybody can squeeze one in. Don't be afraid to go to a class. But try to get a job *first* and see what kind of comments you get from potential employers. If you begin to see a pattern of rejection forming or see that you have no marketable skills, then you can always look into some courses. If you do go to school, ascertain that what you are learning will be very marketable; don't spin your wheels in some class on existential philosophy if what you need is a vocational skill. The esoteric classes can come after you have a job (unless you're working toward a degree and the classes are required). There is nothing worse than taking the time to learn something only to discover that you can't get a job because the field is overcrowded or there is no demand.

The most recent vocational information predicts that in 1990 the largest number of jobs will be available in the fields of storing and retrieving information, as well as in the traditional professions such as attorney, doctor, dentist, and optometrist. Many jobs will be open for computer systems analysts, word processors, and other computer-related workers. There will be less of a need for teachers, however, because the birth rate has fallen. A tremendous need will exist for service-industry personnel, such as waitresses, maids, hotel and motel workers, restaurant workers at all levels, and building maintenance workers, but unfortunately many of these jobs are low-paying. The health professions will continue to need personnel, and will be an almost guaranteed area for jobs.

Also, consider going into business for yourself. If you have skills that people need or interests that could form the nucleus of a business, try to put them to work for you. Many women are taking this route and doing very well.

I have had the experience of failing at a business, so I can give you some advice on how to avoid the pitfalls. My partner and I opened a private office to provide classes and counseling to the community in such areas as alcohol treatment, obesity, parenting skills, and the more traditional marital, family, and individual counseling. Our first mistake was to open in quarters that were too expensive, rather than starting modestly. It is always easier to expand than to contract. Our overhead was too high. We spent too much on advertising, and the office image, including an answering service, gorgeous stationery designed by an artist, professionally executed brochures, and ads in the Yellow Pages. We paid our staff too much. And when clients didn't materialize quickly, we were in a squeeze. In addition, we both held other jobs and couldn't give the business the attention that it needed. So—take a lesson from our sad experience. Start modestly, be appropriately capitalized, devote a lot of attention to your business, and keep your overhead low, if possible.

Operating a business from your own home has many advantages. You can be there for your children, your overhead will be much less, and you can write off part of your home expenses on your income tax. The disadvantage is that you may further isolate yourself from the world and may not meet new people easily, although some home businesses do require you to get out into the community to promote your products or services. These factors must be taken into account, as your work can be a major way to meet men. In Chapter Three, I will give specific advice on using your job to meet men, but let's just say here that it's harder to enlarge your network of people when your work isolates you, and one of the things a single woman *must* do is enlarge her network.

You must also weigh these considerations against the difficulty of getting day care for your children, if they are very young and not yet in school. I'm sure you'll explore all the options, but keep asking around. Good day-care facilities are scarce and can be expensive, and it may take all your ingenuity to find a decent, affordable solution. One woman I know made a deal with her mother. She made her a partner and contracted to pay her a portion of her earnings to care for her children. As her earnings increased and her career took off, the older woman benefited as well, with increased compensation. The deal worked out fine for both parties. They both earned money, the grandmother enjoyed caring for the children, and the mother could pursue her career secure in the knowledge that her children were in loving, competent hands.

If your children are older, they can be very cooperative about sharing chores, chauffering responsibilities, and caring for the younger children. Mine were wonderful.

This just about says it all regarding your looks, money, job and personal life style. Now we're ready to move on and actually *meet* some men.

CHAPTER THREE

How to Meet Men: The Great Adventure

Now you have reevaluated your life and your identity, and started or continued your personal makeover. The next big question might be, "How do I meet men?" Although we *know* that there are more women than men out there in the marketplace of life, we also know that women are meeting and marrying men every day.

Since many women today are leading extremely busy lives, with little time and energy to spare, it is important to keep your eyes open for available men in everyday situations. Don't scatter your energies by looking for men in "all the wrong places." Even in 1939 Dorothy Dix, the advice columnist for the New Orleans *Picayune*, suggested that "fishers of men . . . should use discrimination in picking out the streams in which they fish." You can't expect to find your man in places where your "type" doesn't hang out. If you want a man who doesn't drink, for instance, you obviously shouldn't be frequenting bars. If you hate politics, don't volunteer for a political campaign hoping to meet men—the ones you meet will be political animals. Since older women don't have a lot of time to waste on long-term relationships that go nowhere, choose carefully *before* you enter into a relationship. Don't let a little loneliness tempt you into investing a lot of time with a man who is plainly wrong for you. <u>Anyone who does not actually enhance your life will be one more drain on your energy, time, and emotional resources.</u>

You might also learn to look at the men around you from a different point of view. Contrary to the myth that you "will meet a stranger across a crowded room" and that some instantaneous chemistry will bowl you both over, most relationships take time to develop. Often someone you see every day and take for granted turns out to be a wonderful marriage prospect, once you take the time to get to know him and no longer see him as part of the woodwork. When you begin to think of any unmarried man that you know as a possible love object, all kinds of new possibilities will open up to you. (But be sure he doesn't have a twenty-six-year-old girlfriend from California who visits once a month, as happened to one woman I know.)

But how can I compete? There are so many love-hungry, lonely women out there—many of them gorgeous and aggressive, which I'm not.

Many young, attractive, intelligent women *are* out there competing for the same men. But do you believe that there is *no* man for you in this entire world? That would be ridiculous. Therefore, what you want to advertise to the world is yourself and your own uniqueness. <u>If you are your genuine self, at ease in your own skin, if you convey an aura of liking men and yourself, *and* if you are open to experience—people will respond to that and you will attract some nice men.</u> You're really *not* competing; there's only one of you! And, as they teach in real estate school, all you need is *one* interested buyer!

Also, remember that despite the propaganda in the media, most of the world does not consist of perfect bodies and faces. After the first few minutes, most men agree that faces with radiance and character are more attractive than vapid, flawless faces, and a soft voice and warm, caring manner more important than big breasts.

When you say not to waste your time with inappropriate men, does this mean that every man you spend time with has to be a potential husband?
No. But many women make the mistake of discounting a whole group of men up front before trying them out. For instance, they'll say, "I'll never date a younger man, or a bald man, or a Jewish, Catholic, short, fat, Latin, tall man." Substitute your own prejudice.

This is a self-destructive way to think because a single woman needs many different men in her life for purposes other than romance. I used to joke that I wanted to have five boyfriends—an auto mechanic, a doctor, a dentist, a sugar daddy, and an appliance repairman! I never reached that goal, but here are some real examples of the men who helped make *my* single life interesting and fun.

The Bridge: This is the guy who helps you survive the time between significant relationships. Both of you realize that this isn't a "grand passion," but you like each other well enough to go out to dinner occasionally, or spend a lazy Sunday afternoon in the park, or maybe even go to bed together now and then. It's nice to have the phone ring and know there's someone on the other end who wants your company, even if he isn't Mr. Right.

Because you both feel unpressured, it's easy to talk to this kind of man. You can try out different feminine wiles and learn some important things both about yourself and about men. When you become seriously involved with someone, you can say to this man, "I'm involved with someone right now," and when the new love relationship fizzles, you can call him and take up again where you left off. As long as you don't expect him to change, this kind of relationship has a lot of pluses.

The Younger Man: One of the major shocks to my respectable middle-aged system was that young men pursued me with zeal. At first I found it amusing, and treated them with humor and gentle rebuffs, saying such things as, "I don't know whether to adopt you or date you." My daughters reprimanded me and told me that such remarks were bruising to a man's ego. So I stopped—and decided to be more open-minded. I'm glad I did, because soon I was having a delightful affair with a man over twenty years my junior.

Most people think that older women have affairs with young men for sex and that young men have affairs with older women for money. In my case, as in many others, this wasn't true. I had just ended a long, sexually fulfilling relationship with a man who was sixty, and *I* had little money. This relationship with a younger man was a marvelous learning experience, and it was I who constantly said "no" to marrying him. You can imagine how good I felt about myself as a woman after this involvement, which ended for reasons having nothing to do with age. This loving, intelligent man, who was more mature than many older men, taught me a lot about life and love and helped me open up to all kinds of possibilities. I no longer held rigid ideas about who was an appropriate mate for *anyone,* and I became much less judgmental.

If not for this affair that happened early in my single life, I might also have fallen prey to the diminished self-esteem that many middle-aged women feel when faced with the idea of competing with young women in the man/woman arena. (This is also why I can reassure *you* that you are a desirable woman, no matter what your age.) A woman can feel this age-related insecurity especially where I live, in

South Florida. A certain kind of man abounds here. He is often seen in the chic clubs, sitting at bars and waiting for women to make overtures to him. He is usually middle-aged, well-to-do, fit, successful, and spoiled by young women looking for a rich protector. He refers to women my age as "old bags," while he considers himself a "mature man of the world." Knowing that I was desired by young men, I had an inner serenity and self-confidence about my body and my looks that enabled me to surmount the "old bag" propaganda.

The Older Man: Through my work I met a man who was twenty-two years older than myself, and we had a warm relationship until his death three years ago. He made me feel like a child again, and it made him happy and proud to be seen with me at restaurants and at business meetings. He called me "darling" and told people jokingly that I was his "boss," which technically I was, though he was ten times more affluent than I and smarter by a long shot. We had lovely lunches and dinners together, and long, leisurely conversations on the telephone. He used to tell me that if he were twenty years younger, he would be on my doorstep, which helped me through the times when my love affairs were not going well and my ego was bruised. It was a nonsexual closeness, which is rare between men and women and important to experience. I never asked him for anything or took advantage of his friendship or wealth; it was more important to have him as a friend. He was an important influence on me during this period of experimentation, learning, and living alone.

The Mentor: Other authors have written a great deal about the importance of a mentor. This man can teach you all there is to know about whatever business you're in and can push you into openings in the company as they become available. This can be especially important for an older woman who is just reentering the job market and lacks an established network in the business community. There may be sexual overtones to this relationship, but they should be covert and never consummated, especially if he is married. It is usually up to the woman to keep it that way—otherwise, it will deteriorate into just another bed thing, and you will have lost your business ally if and when the relationship goes sour. (In rare cases, you *can* end up married—but you still will lose your job!) Remember the old adage, "Never sleep where you eat."

The Old Boyfriend: This guy is someone who loved you when you were eighteen, and now you look him up when you go back to your hometown. You dine and reminisce, and find out more about who you were then, and how you became the person you are now. You laugh and talk about the sexual frustrations you endured, and the course your lives have taken. You learn why certain kinds of men continue to attract you, and why he and you never made it. It also helps to know that he never forgot you, and vice versa. Sometimes it becomes a sexual encounter, but only if he is single.

The Old Lover: I was able to remain friends with a few of my old lovers after the affair was over and they married someone else. Many women shy away from such friendships, but they can be very rewarding as long as both of you can tolerate the limits of the relationship. After all, you know each other intimately, and can share problems, hopes, dreams, laughter, and maybe even some harmless flirting. He might even introduce you to new men. My daughters have a real talent for doing this. They still enjoy the company of some of their ex-boyfriends, and count them and their wives among their friends.

Get the idea? A woman needs all kinds of men in her social network. It is important to think of men as friends, not just as lovers or potential mates. As your network expands, you will meet more and more men, and one of them may well be "Mr. Right."

I've met a terrific man who seems interested in me, but unfortunately he's married. He says he's thinking about getting a divorce. Should I throw all caution to the wind and go out with him?
You can be very tempted to do this if there is no other man in your life because you may feel that you will have an ally and a protector in the married man and yet still be free to explore new relationships with available men. I know three women who met their present husbands when one or both of them were married, but despite *their* success at surviving the divorce period and marrying these men, I still can't recommend it. There are too many chances to get hurt or be used. Despite your initial intentions you may fall in love with him and want to marry him. You may waste precious years waiting for a divorce that never comes, or if it does, the man may want to be "free" to explore his options "for a while," and you may be discarded. In addition, it's difficult to bond to a new love when you are emotionally involved with another man, and if he is married you are the one who's taking the big risk. He risks nothing.

Why didn't you meet your "goal" of five boyfriends?
Because I found that it wasn't possible to have a close, meaningful involvement with more than one man at a time. I had visions of single life being the same as it was when I was in my teens and dated four or five men regularly. I had forgotten that in the 1940s, dating did not involve sex and it was not expected. Today, as always, if a man cares about you he doesn't want you going to bed with other men. Al-

so, there's no way for you to conceal the fact that you are dating others, and you jeopardize those nice, spontaneous calls when he asks, "What are you doing? Would you like to meet me for a cup of coffee, a pizza, or a drink?" and you have to say "Sorry, I have other plans." If *you* can handle it, go ahead. I never could. The jealousy and the holding back of feelings that resulted spoiled the trust and honesty that are the basic qualities of a good relationship.

What do men *have to say about meeting* women?

Formerly single men tell me that it is just as hard for them to meet appropriate women as vice versa, although one man was given a list of women to call by a friend when he was divorced and hadn't yet called everyone on it before he remarried five years later. He remarried his former wife, however, so numbers alone don't assure men that they'll meet "Ms. Right."

Men say that we women tend to think that all a man has to do is ask, and women fall into his arms. In reality, many men are shy and insecure, and asking a woman out can be an ordeal. "No man likes to get shot down," one man told me.

So—books have also been written for men on how to meet women. *How to Pick Up Girls* by Eric Weber espouses the theory that any woman may be lonely and just waiting for a man to approach her. In *Singles*, Jacqueline Simenauer and David Carroll report that three-quarters of the women they surveyed said they would be willing to let a man pick them up. However, many of the women doubted they would actually go through with it unless the man met "all their standards." Most men are very much aware of being sized up this way, and so they find it difficult to take Weber's advice and approach strange women in museums, on buses, in health clubs, and in other such places. The men I interviewed said that they seldom tried to pick up women.

It was far more usual for them to meet a woman through business channels, on blind dates, or at parties given by friends—and since *we* are the women men are meeting, these are obviously good methods for us as well.

My male experts emphasize, however, that women should look "approachable." They encourage you to act friendly to the men you encounter at work and play. Even if such men aren't available, they may very well introduce you to someone who is. At the very least, you have enlarged your social network.

How did you meet your husband?
Through "my daughter, the lawyer"! She decided that I needed exposure, and invited me to accompany her to a breakfast for her university law school alumni. There I met Leonard, who immediately impressed me, though we only spoke for a short time. He was brought there by *his* friend, Alan, who happened to be my daughter's associate at the law firm where she worked. When we ambled over to say hello, I had a chance to chat with Leonard.

After the breakfast, I asked my daughter to find out if Leonard was single; she did, and he was. Later, Alan told him that "Aimee's mother liked him" and would like to get to know him better. He called me two weeks later (no one said he was impulsive), and from our first date we were a happy, comfortable pair. By the way, he had never married and was fifty-two years old, so I guess he was ready to meet a nice girl like me! We were married nine months later. This should reassure all you mothers out there that it isn't true that we get no pleasure from our children!

All this is very interesting, but what is really the best way to meet men?
The best way to meet men—and the way that most women meet their husbands—is either through personal introduc-

tions or through their work. Though a few meet through
the other highly touted channels, such as singles groups,
marriage bureaus, travel, participation in sports, going to
museums, and taking classes, the truth is that these methods seldom work. As I said in Chapter One, it's fine to do
these things for their own sake, but don't look upon them
as the key to romance or you will be very disappointed.

This seems to be the appropriate place to discuss the
time-honored "fix-up." It may be necessary for you to *remind* your friends from time to time that you are interested
in this method of meeting men. Without a little prodding
now and then, they may tend to forget about it. It's not that
they don't care—they get involved in their own busy lives,
and assume that we are just as busy.

You should remind your friends that it is *you* they are
fixing up, not the man, so that they keep *your* needs in
mind when they matchmake. You may still meet some totally unsuitable men through these matches, but what have
you really lost if you spend an evening with someone
whose worst fault is that he just doesn't inspire you? If your
friends thought enough of him to introduce you, he can't
be all bad. So think positively whenever you're offered an
intro.

A male veteran of many such encounters agreed with
me when I asked him how *he* felt about it. He didn't mind if
every gal didn't set off rockets. He enjoyed having a dinner
companion because he hated eating alone, and even after a
few disappointing experiences he still preferred this method of meeting women to any other.

I must warn you, though, that if the matchmaking couple chooses to invite you to their home for dinner and you
two are the main course, these evenings can be awkward
for you. I used to beg the hostess to invite other people as
well, to defuse the attention that was focused on the two
victims, but she wouldn't. Instead, she'd sit and beam at us

like a proud hen whose chick had just emerged from the egg. I hated the fact that the man and I both knew that the only reason for the occasion was for us to meet. I could barely look at the poor man openly, lest he think I was sizing him up while I tried to sneak glances while he wasn't watching. However, if the guy was perceptive enough to see past my shyness and the awkwardness of the situation, and if we liked each other, it *was* a good foundation for a relationship. When you meet through introductions, the man is prescreened, and at least you need not be afraid that he's a looney.

One of my long relationships began when I went alone to a New Year's Eve party at the home of a close married friend. She was one of those angelic creatures who included her single friends when she gave a party. One of the other guests mentioned to her that he had just come from a mutual friend's party, which reminded my friend that the other host was single. She invited us both to dinner, and we were off!

The next best way to meet men is through your work, especially if you have a job that puts you in daily contact with a lot of them. Working with men provides a gradual way of getting to know someone before you become romantically involved, which is an ideal situation. Take a fresh look at the men around you in your workplace. You may perceive that the guy you take for granted, and who you think is married or has a girlfriend, is as lonely as you are. If you're attracted to someone at work, talk to him once in a while. You can drop hints that you find him attractive, and hope that he will take the initiative and ask you out. Otherwise you can always invite *him* to something so he can see you in a different setting, not just as a co-worker. You might ask him to go to a party with you, for example.

One previously married lady met her future husband when she hired *him* to work for *her*. They were just friends and co-workers until they both went away to the same seminar in another state. That weekend gave them a new perception of each other, and they fell in love. They have been happily wed now for thirteen years.

I worked in a job that guaranteed that I would never meet anyone eligible. I was the director of a federally funded job training agency that taught indigent Haitian and Hispanic immigrants to speak English. My clients were poor and uneducated, and my co-workers mostly young or married. My salary was very good, however, and I couldn't afford to change jobs just to meet men. Fortunately, I had some friends and contacts outside the workplace to make up for the lack of opportunity on the job.

If you can afford to change jobs, put yourself in a setting where you meet a lot of people, not just single men, who can enlarge your social network. Some such jobs are receptionist, health-club employee, hospital worker, adult education instructor, boat rental desk or golf pro shop employee, hotel gift shop employee, waitress, and restaurant hostess, as well as the traditional professions. Even the women you meet may have a brother or cousin who is single, and the married men can still introduce you to someone even though *they* aren't available.

A note of caution about the infamous office affair. Although the latest thinking on the subject casts a more favorable light on "amour" in business, you must still be extremely discreet. If an affair goes sour between people on different levels of management, usually the one in the inferior position is asked to leave the job. Too often, this is the woman. However, there is no reason not to fall in love with someone you meet in the workplace. Just try not to flaunt your sexual interest. Save the soulful glances and caresses for after five. It's important to maintain a businesslike attitude on the job at all times, rather than give management an excuse to reprimand you for not keeping your mind on your work.

Romantic liaisons can get even stickier when they involve a secretary and her boss. I remember my first office job "way back when," where a boss and a secretary were playing flirty-poo across their desks. I left the job before I ever learned the outcome of this passionate fling, but I think that I'm pretty safe in assuming that eventually the lady had to leave, as the boss was married. I do know how it affected the rest of the workers, however, and it was "condition negative." The other women in the office felt embarrassed, as though they were invading someone's privacy, and the secretary lost status in everyone's eyes for having no dignity. Footnote: Several women that I met did marry their bosses, though, so such office affairs *can* work out if you use your head and handle yourself intelligently.

Business lunches and seminars also provide a fertile meeting ground for men and women. Although many of the participants are married, there are always some single and divorced men around. Keep your eyes and ears open. Often you are seated randomly at lunch at these seminars, and you can meet people you would not encounter otherwise. So, when the notices come around the office announcing meetings and workshops at which attendance is optional, always ask that you be allowed to go. Rusty says—"She who stays put will not meet men."

What about going to bars? You hear so much about the horrors of singles bars, especially for the older woman.
You can use the bar scene if you don't let it use you! We all have those times, when we are between relationships or just feeling lonely and isolated, when plain old human interaction is what we need. It's all a matter of your expectations. If you go expecting to meet your dream man, you'll be miserable. But if you can go out to a bar just to have fun, you can have some interesting adventures to chuckle over.

Rule #1: Try to go with a girlfriend. It helps to have company on these forays into the wilds. She should be someone who won't cling, be jealous, or mind if you leave earlier or later than she, and whom you enjoy being with even if you don't meet men. I was lucky to have D., who is attractive, fun, intelligent, and who could laugh at the ridiculous along with me when it happened—as it often did. (She was also magnetic to men, and we rarely lacked companionship!) Some women feel that a woman alone is more approachable than two, but I believe that it is more interesting to go with someone else on these outings.

Rule #2: Use your own transportation. This avoids problems if your friend wants to leave earlier or later than you. Sometimes one of you is having a good time and the other is bored and tired. If you have your own transportation, such as separate cars, you are free to go home when you like.

Rule #3: Never—and I mean *never*—give your phone number to, or go home with, a man you meet in a bar. If he's an interesting possibility, tell him why you can't give him your telephone number when he asks for it (these dangerous times, etc.) and take *his* number. If, in the light of day, you still want to see him again, *you* can call *him*. I never met a man who minded this, and many enjoyed the intrigue.

It's a fascinating experiment in human behavior to see the insecurity this simple move can evoke in a seemingly together man. Often they would say with a crestfallen look, "You'll never call." Well, I *did* call one or two, but none proved interesting over the long term—which may say something about the effects of good music, dim lights, and a drink or two.

This brings us to **Rule #4:** *Never drink too much.* (A.) A drunk woman is most unattractive and unfeminine. (B.) You have to drive yourself home—or at least take yourself home on public transportation. (C.) You don't want to end up going home with or to his hotel room with some guy you might not even speak to in "real life"!

With these cautions and helpful hints under your belt, you can now try the bar scene with a whole new outlook. On some of those Friday nights when I was dateless, it saved my soul to go to a place where there was music and a bar, where I could dance for hours, drink a little, flirt, and reject men or not, just as I did in my teens at the local "Y" dances.

You should know, though, that sometimes I left feeling more depressed and lonely than before. *Expect this also.* Some nights the mood will be wrong, the place empty, or everyone else paired off, and you may feel more alone than ever. Knowing this in advance can help a little, but be prepared to have some hard moments when you feel that you'd run off into the sunset with the first man who has clean nails and asks you to. *DON'T!* The mood will pass, daylight will come, and a brisk walk in the sun or a workout on the tennis court or at the gym will soon restore your spirits, and your life will flow on.

What about those ads in the personal columns? I know some people are using them, but I can't shake the idea that only desperate people or losers would resort to such a tactic.
Well, kiddo, as Ann Landers loves to say, "Wake up and smell the coffee!" While you're sitting home worrying about losers, some really smart people out there are having the time of their lives. A recent issue of *New York* magazine did an in-depth article on the growing popularity of personal ads. It seems that the people who advertise are no longer just "weirdos and losers." Many of them are young and older professionals looking for love and marriage. They even refer to the people they meet as the ones "your mother wanted you to bring home." According to *New York,* theorists see the growth of this phenomenon as related to the Old West custom of advertising for brides, be-

cause, like the men of old, if you're busy forging ahead in the world you don't have time to go looking for a mate. And when you do have time, where can you go? Church socials? Bars? The chances of meeting someone compatible at such places are very slim, while advertising your needs can immediately bring you a wide selection of people to choose from. The article goes on to say that one recent ad in New York's *Village Voice* brought a woman responses from "four surgeons, ten lawyers, five college professors, two media executives, two journalists, and one foreign policy expert." If nothing else, these advertisers are meeting people.

Some women even exchange the phone numbers and names of their respondents or pool their money for one ad. They have the leisure to sit back and read the replies in the comfort and safety of their living rooms and to evaluate how the man sounds. It's fun to write an ad and even more fun to get all the mail, even if you decide not to reply to anyone. You remain completely anonymous, as the replies go to a box number at the publication and then are forwarded to you. The consensus is that most people live up to their descriptions, and that if you meet on neutral ground, where you can leave gracefully if you don't like each other, there is little danger. *New York Magazine* says that this method is certainly as safe as picking someone up at any large gathering of people.

The article does mention certain code words to watch out for, however, such as "Rubenesque" (fat), "living simply" (broke), and "sensual" (wants to have sex on the first date). It also states that men send the most letters and place the most ads, and that the average woman receives forty replies; the average man, fifteen.

Since *I* was too chicken and too dumb to use this method when I was single, I decided to experiment with it now, as I didn't want to espouse something I hadn't tried myself. I wrote an ad for a single fortyish female friend of mine and placed it in the largest newspaper in our area, which has a very small personals section. They had restrictions for the ad; no photos or biographies could be requested, and you had to mention two points of interest, such as "likes fishing and sailing." The ad cost $45.00 and ran for three days. It stated, among other things, that she was a "40s female who likes conversation and dancing," but included no details about physical appearance.

My friend received thirty-six replies, of which she will follow up on about eight. The professions represented were lawyer, engineer, stockbroker, businessman, teacher, social worker, and psychologist. If I were single, I would have explored four of those replies.

I was amazed at the forthrightness of the men and the lack of any need to hide their identity. Many enclosed photos, some sent printed resumes, many used their business letterhead, and none were obscene or off-color in any way. Many of the letters were very open and expressive of their need for someone with whom to share their already happy lives. The age range was amazing, from twenties and thirties to fifties and sixties, as well as one college student.

I'm now completely sold on this method for meeting men, and am sorry that I had a poor attitude about it as a single. It would have made my life even more exciting and adventurous. My friend is now busy following up, which should keep her occupied for months!

Most experts feel that you should place your ad in a publication that reaches the kind of people in whom you would be interested. Since not many publications carry these ads, your local newspaper would be a good place to start. Try to write an ad that's cute, different, and attention-getting. One local woman was recently written up in our newspaper because she had just broken up with her boyfriend, and placed an ad to say so and to announce that she was sad and needed company. She was swamped with re-

plies. Give it a try and see how it works out. You have nothing to lose!

The *New York Review of Books* has traditionally carried
the most imaginative ads, and the *Village Voice* is another famous source. I recently subscribed to a newsletter for singles published in Florida, which features ads *only* from men
and women looking for mates. There are a few token fea-
ture articles, but the entire publication, which costs seventeen dollars for a yearly subscription, is devoted primarily
to ads. In the April 1984 issue, I counted 93 ads placed by
men and 102 placed by women. Many of them were placed
by physicians, lawyers, and other professional persons of
both sexes. So there *are* men out there who are willing to
advertise at a cost of up to fifty dollars for the opportunity
to meet a compatible lady. This magazine also lists singles
events in the area and different organizations for singles
who might care to join. These run the gamut from social organizations to religious groups to special-interest groups
such as sailing, skiing, camping, and of course Parents
Without Partners, the granddaddy of them all.

*Have you also looked into the matchmaking services and
dating bureaus?*
Yes. I also followed up on some ads in the paper that were
placed by dating services. One advertised "zodiac introductions." When I inquired, the director assured me that
since it was my birth month, I would get a 50 percent discount. His method of doing business was to make a visit to
your home "to be sure that you were serious and not married, so that he could make a referral with some authority."
Then he would take a photo of you, and after two weeks
you would be in their file. After that they gave a first name,
phone number, and photo to a man and to you, and who
called whom would be up to the clients. You could exclude
any zodiac sign that you wished. They also sponsored boat

trips, cruises, and travel, and put out a bimonthly newsletter. The annual fee was a whopping $375. My feeling about this operation was that it was a bit sleazy and dangerous, and more interested in making money than in helping individuals to meet appropriate people. Beware of these kinds of second-rate services, and be very discreet before you use any service.

Another dating service that I investigated claimed to be in its twelfth year of operation. The manager claimed that he had a "customized program" wherein you could sign up for one month, three months, or one year. There was an initial interview, for which there was no charge. He, too, reiterated that many men in his files were deeply involved in their business or profession and had little leisure time. They wanted to meet women, but didn't know where to go and in any case had little time to go anywhere.

This service seemed a little more legitimate, though the man wouldn't quote costs over the telephone. Some people have had good results from using such services.

Another service catered to Jewish clients and was run by a psychologist. She charged $300 a year and guaranteed four introductions. If you married, she expected a bonus. This lady showed me some of the photos of people in her files; they looked attractive and had good credentials. As an added fillip, she found herself a new husband when he came to her bureau as a client.

A new trend is for nonprofit religious and religiously based organizations to form matchmaking services of their own, which is an example of an old Eastern European and Asian custom making a comeback. Several large Jewish organizations have already initiated such services, and New York is about to begin one under the auspices of the New York Federation of Jewish Philanthropies. According to their publicity, the program is aimed at "lonely, high-achieving young Jews," and was originally the brainchild of a rabbi who said he was "fed up with 'ripoff' dating services that are more concerned with making money from singles than making matches."

In a number of other countries, the government considers it their responsibility to bring people together. The government of Japan, for instance, traditionally ran picnics for single people for the sole purpose of matchmaking. The men and the women shot arrows into an oversized disc with numbers printed on it. The man and woman who held the same number were then introduced for the purpose of marriage, and the government stepped aside and let nature take its course in this lottery of love.

Lacking such institutionalized methods in this country, we have to be more ingenious!

What have other women done to meet men?
I asked some remarried women how they had handled this aspect of singleness. Here are some representative replies.

> QUESTION: What kinds of things did you try in order to meet men?

> ANSWERS: "Attended singles club meetings."
>
> "Told people I was single and interested in meeting men."
>
> "Joined clubs and attended meetings (professional, ski club, etc.)."
>
> "Took a job in a place where there would be an opportunity to run into single men."
>
> "Went to social functions related to institutions with which I was involved, like the United Way."

"Spent time at the gym."

"Took classes at the university."

"Met men through other single and married friends and relatives."

"Went to singles bars."

QUESTION: What methods for meeting men did you eventually discard because you felt that they were useless?

ANSWERS: "Singles clubs."

"Bars."

"Singles dances."

QUESTION: How did you meet your husband?

ANSWERS: "Through introduction by family."

"Introduction."

"At a mutual friend's house at a party."

"Through an introduction by his cousin."

"He was investigating a robbery and I was visiting the victim."

"I was a travel agent and I met him on an official trip."

"On a trip abroad."

"We worked together."

"Blind date."

"His children were friends with my children and told him to call me."

"We met at a singles bar where we were fighting over the same stool."

"He was a doctor, and I came to his office as a patient."

"I remarried my previous husband."

"His friends introduced us."

"I was his employee and we disliked each other for a long time, until he asked me out to dinner one night."

I would like to sum up by encouraging you to do two things. One is to go out as often as you have the opportunity, even if you feel depressed and it's an effort to drag yourself out. You never know what adventure is waiting around the corner.

The second is to think differently about who is actually a marriage prospect for you. In Chapter One, I discussed the marriage squeeze in terms of the discrepancy in the numbers of available men and women of certain ages. For far too long, women have felt that they had to marry someone who was older, taller, richer, better or as well educated as they, and from a comparable or better social class. This is no longer practical in today's world. There *is* no man shortage if you discard some of these archaic ideas. For instance, I know several women who support their husbands financially. They don't mind. They're women of means and they love their husbands dearly—they're very happy. I also know lonely, wealthy women who have no lovers or husbands because they are obsessed with the idea that the man for them has to be rich enough to support them. Isn't this sad when you think about it? (But do heed my cautions in Chapter Six about the "gold digger.")

Think in terms of falling in love with someone who

may be different from the "ideal" you formulated in your mind when you were sixteen or reading romance novels. There are many loving, delightful men in this world who may be younger than you, or have less education, or work at jobs that may not have status. Maybe he can't quote Shakespeare. So what? You can go to a study group to discuss the great Bard—your husband doesn't have to fill all your needs. Women must get comfortable with the idea of "loving down." No one looks askance at the famous male trial lawyer when he marries a gorgeous girl who never completed High School, who works as a waitress, and whose family is the modern day equivalent of horsethieves! So why should *you* worry about these things? If a guy is loving with you and cares about you . . . if you can talk to each other . . . if you enjoy being together . . . if you hold the same values . . . if you are happy with each other—don't worry about what "people" will think, not even your family or children. Do what *you* need to do to be happy. Try not to get frozen into stereotypical ideas about the kind of men you should allow yourself to know, or you'll close off a lot of good opportunities for happiness.

In summary, here are my ideas for meeting men:

1. Use discrimination in picking out the "streams in which you fish."

2. Learn to look at the men around you in a different way—as prospective spouses.

3. Don't worry about competing. If you are your genuine self, someone will respond to you.

4. There is not just *one* man for you in this world, there are many. Get that idea out of your head.

5. Don't discount a whole group of men before trying them out.

6. Don't get involved with married men.

7. Have other men in your life, not just "grand passions."

8. Remember that it's just as hard for men to meet nice women as for women to meet nice men.

9. Keep in touch with your friends as they will fix you up.

10. Try to use your job as a way to meet men.

11. Use the singles bar scene for what it is—a way to have an interesting evening and let your hair down.

12. Try the personal ads. They're fun and *they work*.

13. Try dating services if you wish, but watch out for disreputable or dangerous agencies.

14. Go out if you're invited. You never know if this will be the one, and the most you'll lose is an evening. No one meets anyone sitting at home alone.

15. Have fun! Don't take all this too seriously.

Now let's move on to everything I know about sex.

CHAPTER FOUR

The Sexual Connection: What's Right For You

L et's eavesdrop on a group of single women over forty talking about men. Inevitably one will say, "Who needs them? They only want *one thing*." (No one has to ask what the one thing is; they all *know*.) "They take you out to dinner and expect you to go to bed with them." This usually accompanies another complaint: "What do I need a husband for? Who wants to wash a man's underwear again anyway?"

I feel that these kinds of comments are self-defeating. They're usually made by a woman who doesn't have a man in her life, doesn't know how to find one, and has resigned herself to that fact. She has convinced herself that these thoughts express what she really feels.

Even younger women think this way, but they'll say, "Men are jerks. They're only interested in sex. If you go to bed with them they drop you, and if you don't, they say you're frigid. It's still a man's world. All they care about is themselves and their needs. Don't they know that I'm a person, with emotional needs as well as a body? Men think with their penises" (or whatever word they use to describe that particular organ!).

87

Women in their twenties and thirties have to deal with
men who have been socialized within the new morality,
which means "You do your own thing and I'll do mine,"
sexual freedom, the pill, and "I need my space."

But women in their forties and fifties were brought up
to save themselves for "Mr. Right," who was going to carry
them off into the sunset to live happily ever after. Well,
here you are without a husband for one reason or another,
and back on the dating scene, feeling a little misplaced. Perhaps you had one sex partner for most of your life or if you
did stray, it was probably just a hurried, harried happening
once or twice and not a wild love affair. It may have taken
years of marriage to overcome the prohibitions you were
brought up with, if you ever did. Now that you're single
again, you may find that you still think of men as lascivious
creatures ready to pounce on you when your guard is
down.

Well, I've been out there in the singles world, and I can
reassure you. This is not true of the mature men you mostly
will be dealing with. The older man knows something
about women because he has usually been involved with
one or two by this time. In my experience, he is a considerate and caring lover. He is not in a hurry and he knows how
to woo his woman. He is also slowing down sexually, although he would never admit it. For years the literature has
been reminding us that a woman's sexual desires peak in
her late twenties and early thirties and remain constant
throughout life, whereas a man's peak at about age sixteen.
After that his powers gradually decline, usually reaching a
plateau that continues throughout life *if* he remains sexually active.

Many men, however, become so involved in their life's
work that they neglect their sexual side until they become
single again and have to interact with women once more.
They may need a lot of reassurance even to *have* a sexual ex-

perience. Even the men who push and nag and try to get you into bed from the first date may turn out to be impotent once you're finally in bed together. So don't be afraid of the sexual aspect of the husband search. If you're careful about whom you date, it can be one of the most interesting and fulfilling aspects of your single life.

What do I do first?

One of the first things you have to do is crystallize your own individual philosophy, the one by which you have lived comfortably until now. If you are deeply religious or conservative by nature, for instance, you won't be comfortable in a sexual relationship that does not include commitment. Trying to act in a way that is not consistent with your beliefs will only depress you and turn you off to men and sex. Each of us has to find her sexual niche. This is not to say that you can't modify your outlook through your experiences, but I want to point out that it's OK if you don't or can't. We are living in a society that is sexually free at the present, and it's easy to feel out of step; but don't forget that sexual freedom includes the right to say "no" or "not yet." Remember when I said earlier that if you're your genuine self someone out there will appreciate it? Well, it's true about sex, too. There *are* men who share your beliefs and who take sex seriously. They consider it an important decision, not to be made carelessly or thoughtlessly.

On the other hand, if you feel you've been seriously restricted in your wish to explore your sexuality, and if you're eager for sexual adventure and experience—this is OK, too. We all know that life is not endless and that we won't be around forever. I often say that when I'm sitting in my rocking chair with my memories on the porch of the nursing home, I want to be smiling.   ✗

By now, you are a woman experienced in decision making. You know what makes you feel happy and comfortable with yourself, and what does not. Apply these same standards to sex and you won't go wrong.

I would like to be more sexually free—any suggestions as to how I can do this?
If you do decide to go to bed with a man, think of it this way. Sex is not something that you give away and that's lost forever. Like a smile, there's always more where it came from. Sexual needs recur again and again, unless they have been deeply repressed. Like many things, the sex drive seems to be self-perpetuating; frequent sex leads to the desire for frequent sex. To put it less delicately, for both men and women the battle cry is "use it or lose it." There may, of course, be periods in your life when you must live without sexual relations for one reason or another. You survive that, too. Often during those times the sex drive lessens through some primal adaptive mechanism. Of course, masturbation can help, and many experts advocate it as a means of keeping sexuality alive when you don't have a partner.

It should come as no surprise to you that women need sex, too. But we also need cuddling, touching, stroking, and talking. The desire to be touched goes back to a basic human need that originates in infancy, when we can actually die without it. This need, known as "skin hunger," was first noted by a man named Rene Spitz, who observed that infants were dying for inexplicable reasons in a well-run foundling home, although they were cleaned and fed properly. However, no one ever held them or cuddled them. The infants did not thrive, and fell into a depressed state termed "anaclitical depression." They just wasted away and died. When the caregivers of this institution made an effort to hold each infant during feeding and to "bond" with them, the deaths no longer occurred.

For us as adults this means that without touching, hugging, cuddling, or stroking we shrivel up in our souls.

Sometimes a woman makes a trade-off and goes to bed with someone just for the closeness she needs. Often she feels guilty and rotten about it afterward and gives herself all kinds of negative messages about her self-worth. But why browbeat yourself? You should be allowed to satisfy your needs without feeling guilty or diminished!

At other times we need good old-fashioned down-home sex for sex's sake. This is also a valid reason to go to bed with someone. If a man attracts you and if you need him that day, I say go ahead and do it, keeping in mind what I said earlier about your personal convictions. You are not giving anything away. You are involved in a mutually loving experience. Whether or not you have an orgasm (more on this subject later), sex with a loving man is a soul-satisfying experience. However, if you do go to bed with someone and it is disappointing, you are not diminished and you are not cheapened. You are simply a worthy human being who made an adult choice based on your life experience and your assessment of your needs. Taking the opportunity to have a kind, loving experience need not be cause for recriminations.

I agree, but I'm not sure about how to conduct myself.
What if I seem awkward or foolish?
You may feel self-conscious at first. This is to be expected. As I point out in my chapter on dating, you may very well louse up the first few times and not do everything right. So what? He ain't perfect, either. As for your body, if things have progressed far enough for you to take off your clothes, you can be sure that he finds you physically attractive. We women are painfully aware of every stretch mark, every patch of cellulite, and every wayward lump and bump. But even women with mastectomies and other physical limitations have been pleasantly surprised to discover that sex partners are available. Your man is not going

to subject you to a microscopic examination. Half the time the room is dim, his glasses are off, and he doesn't see so well, anyhow! Besides, chances are *he* has love handles around his waist and a paunch, and wears dentures or a toupee.

Back to basics. I know that you're concerned about the logistics of getting to that moment of truth when you're actually in bed with a new man. Who unbuttons what? Who does what first?

The best advice I ever got on this subject came from a close friend. When I went on my first date as a newly single woman she said, "Let him handle it. He's experienced with women. You just relax and let him take the lead." Sure enough, that's what always happened. When a man wanted to kiss me or seduce me, believe me, he knew how to go about it. I could say "no" if it wasn't what I wanted at the moment—but if it was, it was easy to follow his lead. This is not to say that I was never shy or self-conscious, especially with a new partner, but <u>I learned how to master my fears. So can you, if your expectations are realistic.</u> Don't think you have to perform like the wild young things in magazines, movies, and TV shows. Most of life is not like that. Most people are average, with average looks, average sex drives, and average needs. Everyone is not a sexual athlete, repeating all the moves of the latest sex manual in living color!

What do most women have to say about their sex life after they become single again?
The maturing of a woman's sex drive in her later years, when she is capable of deeper desires and would like to be more experimental, can coincide with unlucky times. Perhaps her marriage is rocky or her sex life has become routine because her spouse is not interested in exploring new avenues of sex.

When a woman becomes newly single, she has a chance to open up this side of her nature and experiment with partners who are more sexually free. She can allow herself to be more uninhibited, and she can get a feeling of renewed attractiveness as a woman. She may project a sensuality about her that never existed before. To be involved in a passionate love affair in her later years can reveal an aspect of her sexuality that a woman might never have known, had it not been for the circumstances that thrust her out into the world again.

So most women are grateful for the opportunity to rediscover themselves as sexual persons, and delighted to find that they are exciting sex partners!

What if I like a man, but he turns out to be disappointing when we go to bed?
The latest technology of sex emphasizes the importance of partners communicating with each other about their intimate needs, but it's difficult to do that even in the best of circumstances and inappropriate when you're not in a close, committed relationship. A relative stranger has no investment in pleasing you, and if you expect that he will, you will be disappointed. Writing a road map of your body for a new man is a turn-off. ("Turn right here, slow down there, watch out for curves.") Later on, when you are closer emotionally, it will be different.

What does this mean?
It means that sometimes you may be giving and caring sexually and not get it back. It means that you may feel loving and concerned about someone and he won't feel the same way about you. It means that sometimes you won't have an orgasm. You have two choices. You can stop associating with this man and write him off as a potential mate, or you can wait and be patient to see if things improve or change

over time. Again, relationships take time! You can't count on instant rapport. Sex with a new partner always improves with practice.

But before you make your decision, I would like to share with you what *I* think is important in a sexual relationship. I think it's great if you can *talk* to the person you're in bed with. I think it's great if you can *laugh* with that person and have fun. I think it's great if you can be tender together, and care about each other's needs. "Techniques" can always be improved if these other factors are present.

Can we discuss the female orgasm?

Yes. We now know that women have a greater orgasmic capacity than men, and are even capable of multiple orgasms. We also know that it takes longer for a woman to reach orgasm and that she is more easily distracted by what is going on around her. The brain is still the most important sexual organ.

My first sexual relationship with a man other than my husband of twenty-eight years was with a man who was giving, loving, and sexually experienced. It took me four (yes, *four*) months of relatively frequent sex to feel free enough to have an orgasm. What was wrong? It had nothing to do with technique, physical attributes, or loving feelings. It had to do with unconscious prohibitions and my need to overcome beliefs that I had internalized during my formative years. I needed to trust this man and to feel free enough to let myself experience orgasm outside marriage. Fortunately, I didn't give up the relationship, and he was understanding enough not to force the issue. Eventually things happened without being forced. *Never* let a man accuse you of frigidity because you don't have an orgasm with him. I also wish to suggest that sex without orgasm can be satisfying for other reasons, such as intimacy or closeness, although sex alone does not guarantee an intimate relationship.

If you have never experienced orgasm, now is the time for you to gain some knowledge and understanding of how your body works. Many books have been written for women about sex, and some have been written by women. *The Hite Report* by Shere Hite tells how women really feel about sex and what they do about it. I suggest you read it to help you realize that <u>anything sexual you may feel has been felt by other women as well</u>.

What if a man I'm interested in has a sex problem? What should I do?

Much of the new research on sex confirms that men and women are more alike sexually than they are different. They go through the same stages of arousal, although the timing may be different. The main difference is that a man must "perform" by producing an erection and keeping it long enough to satisfy his partner. Although a man may act very knowledgeable and sexually secure, he may be quite fearful about his adequacy as a lover, the size of his penis, or the quality of his performance. He may be somewhat afraid of the new woman and her expectations. Mental health professionals use the term "performance anxiety" to describe a man's fear about his ability to perform sexually. He may feel that every other man is adequate, sure of himself, and a great lover because men rarely share their sexual insecurities with each other. They usually bluff or lie about their sexual prowess and pretend that they're studs, whether they are or not.

This is where patience and understanding can go a long way. I found that a man is sometimes impotent when he has just come out of a long relationship with one woman and has to relate to a new one. He becomes habituated to one woman, and she is the one who signals arousal to his brain. If this happens, give him some time and be especially reassuring—it's embarrassing for him to fail. Sometimes you need many experiences together before he returns to his potent self. If you like him and want to continue the relationship, give it a fair chance. Take advantage of the fact that older men are more potent in the mornings than at night, and plan some of your lovemaking for that time. Most men who are not physiologically impotent because of health or medication awaken with an erection in the morning, so this is really a good time to initiate sex.

If you're still having problems after about six tries, you may then decide whether you want to wait while he works out his problem with a therapist, or to end the relationship. Sometimes a man is so kind and loving that a woman doesn't care that he can't have intercourse, and sometimes a man who can produce an erect penis at will is unfeeling, manipulative, and unloving. Consider all your options carefully, and even talk it over with a professional counselor if you wish before you discount a man with a sexual problem as a potential mate. (See Chapter Six for the exceptions to this advice.)

Masters and Johnson have shown that impotence is correctable. If the man chooses to seek professional help, make sure it is with a counselor who specializes in this problem. The professional should be well recommended by a physician or by someone with first-hand knowledge of his competence and reputation in the community. An ethical, professional sex therapist does *not* have sex with his or her patients. A few, however, do use the services of a surrogate partner for the man when no woman is available to work with him.

There are so many myths about men and sex! If you want information, I recommend *Free and Female* by Barbara Seaman and *What Every Woman Should Know About Men* by

Joyce Brothers. For technique, *The Joy of Sex* by Alex Comfort is a good manual.

Any other tips you can give me on how to conduct myself?
Try to remain a little mysterious about sex. Don't seem "professional." One man I interviewed told me about his sexual encounter with a woman he had fantasized about for years. He felt that sex with her would be the ultimate experience. After she divorced, she looked him up, and they went to dinner and ended up in bed. What do you think his complaint was? She was "too good." She knew "all the moves." She showed her whole bag of tricks (if you'll pardon the expression), and he was turned off.

Was he a nut? No. He was saying that a man still likes to feel that he is the pursuer, the one who arouses and gently leads his lady during sex. He does *not* want to feel like man #248. He may know that he isn't the first man she has slept with, but he *would* like to feel that he is special. Keep a balance between spontaneity, know-how, reserve, and passion, and you can't go wrong. It's not so difficult as it sounds.

How can I handle my fear of getting pregnant?
If you are still fertile and if he hasn't had a vasectomy, you will have to do some thinking beforehand about contraception. Talk with your gynecologist and make an informed decision; you do not want the fear of pregnancy to interfere with the spontaneity of your relationships. If your religious beliefs prevent you from taking precautions, you must also do some thinking about that and establish a philosophy about your sex life. Though we would like to think that things have changed and that birth control is the man's responsibility as much as ours, we are still the ones who get

pregnant. *We* are stuck with the consequences if we don't think this matter through.

I've read and heard so much about sexually transmitted diseases. How can I keep from getting one?
You must take precautions; sexually transmitted diseases are epidemic these days. Read up on the subject and discuss it with your doctor.

Some books are on the market that discuss herpes and AIDS (autoimmune deficiency syndrome), the newest sex-related scourges. AIDS seems to be transmitted by the blood or the bodily excretions through a break in the skin, or by blood transfusion from an infected person. It is most prevalent right now among homosexuals, and anal sex appears to be implicated in making one vulnerable. Other groups at high risk for this disease are Haitians, intravenous drug users, and hemophiliacs. This disease attacks the immune system and leads to death from illnesses that the body can no longer fight, such as cancer or pneumonia.

Herpes causes a visible rash on a man's or woman's genitals or in the surrounding area, when the disease is in the active stage. It may resemble pimples surrounded by pink areas, but may also look different. The rash comes and goes, and it is currently believed that when there is a remission and the sores disappear, you are at little risk of becoming infected.

One of the only ways to determine whether a man has active herpes or genital warts (another venereal disease) is to look. Another way is to ask. As mentioned above, however, there are no visible signs when herpes is not in the active phase. The same is true for many of the other venereal diseases, such as syphilis and gonorrhea in the initial stages. Asking someone can be uncomfortable and embarrassing, and you may be lied to. Looking may not always be feasible. About all you can do is to be choosy about who you have sexual relations with.

If a man wears a condom, you are relatively safe from syphilis and gonorrhea but not from herpes, as herpes can infect a larger area than just the genitals. Try to avoid having sex with men who you know have multiple sex partners. These men are more susceptible to diseases. Try to know a man before you bed down with him, and know where he lives so that you can locate him if you need to. Go for gynecological examinations at least twice a year and whenever you have any reason to suspect that you've been infected. But don't panic. Itching and discharge from the vagina can also be symptomatic of minor yeast infections or a fungus, both of which are normal female maladies. You may also have hemophilus or Gardnerella vaginitis, less serious sexually transmitted infections.

Concern about disease has led many men and women to forego sexual relations altogether, but others do not wish to be celibate. It is a difficult and precarious situation for today's single woman, and you will need all your know-how to deal with this problem.

I hope that this chapter has answered some of your questions about how to handle your sexual needs in your search for a new husband. What I have said here is in no way the last word on the subject; you will find many of your own answers. As you become more comfortable with single life and its sexual aspects, you will enjoy your relationships with men more, and sex will become one of your criteria for selection of a new life partner. It is encouraging to note that most remarried people say their sexual relationships are much better the second time around because they have grown freer, more experienced, and more comfortable with their sexuality.

CHAPTER FIVE

Dating:
Pleasures
and Pitfalls

I mperfect as it is, dating is still the primary way most men and women have for getting to know one another. Courting is courting, in any time or culture. Even in the animal kingdom there are established rituals for courtship and mating—but in the natural state it's usually the male who flaunts his plumage and dances around!

Once you're in an established relationship, dating becomes more informal. You'll watch TV together, he'll accompany you to family gatherings, or you'll meet for an impromptu cup of coffee or a drink. But initially we must all go through the traditional dating routine. In the beginning, it is a time of learning and gaining experiences. After a divorce, many people go through a candy-store phase, dating frantically and feverishly, sometimes every night. Eventually, though, they calm down and settle into a more realistic way of life.

I feel so out of touch with that whole scene! I dread it. I don't even know how to act anymore, even though I must admit that the thought of meeting new men is exciting!
It is exciting! But if you're worried about how to cope with

dating after being married and out of practice—take heart,
even though it *is* scary at first. I botched up the first few
times I dated (after twenty-eight years in limbo) and you
may, too. I *really* didn't know how to act. My last date had
been in 1950, the modern-day equivalent of the Stone Age.
I had heard about the new morality, doing your own thing,
and swinging sex, but had no first-hand experience. I felt
awkward and shy, and was afraid my date would think that
I was overeager—and so I withdrew and came across as
aloof. Looking back, I realize these men must have felt that
I didn't like them. But no one died and the earth didn't stop
rotating.

It's perfectly OK if you feel strange at first. Think of
your first dates as similar to making waffles. *You usually
have to throw the first away!* So what? The only way to become comfortable with dating is to do it. Soon you'll find
yourself very much at home in the dating game. You'll be
relaxed and comfortable just being yourself. You'll even *enjoy* it!!

*Are the problems a single woman encounters in today's
world different from those a few years ago?*
Yes, some are. One would have to wear blinders and ear-
plugs to avoid learning about the dangers that exist today.
We *do* have to be more aware of our personal security in our
homes, our comings and goings, and when we date. A
good rule is never to get into a car with, or go home with,
any man that you meet without a reference from someone,
and that includes that nice guy that you meet on the beach,
at the laundromat, or in your pottery class. There are too
many crazies out there preying on women for you to take a
chance and relax this rule, even once. Always have your
first few encounters with such men in public places, such
as a restaurant, and use your own transportation. One per-
sonable man, recently in the headlines, managed to kill

lovely young women all across the United States by promising them photo sessions and a modeling career. He looked presentable and had money and a nice car, but was a certifiable psychopath. Even during the tremendous publicity while he was being hunted, he managed to entice and kill more women.

After you have met the first few times in public places, you can feel fairly safe in inviting your date to pick you up at your home or going to his, but there are still no guarantees. Someone should know his name and telephone number when you plan to be alone with him. I used to call one of my grown daughters when I went out with a new man. I gave her his name and whatever other information I had about him. Then I would call her when I got home, or when he left, to let her know I was OK. I know this sounds juvenile, but on the other hand, I never had any frightening experiences. It's like the old "elephants in New York" joke, which goes like this. A man was standing on a corner in New York City, making strange gestures. A passer-by asked, "Why are you doing that?" The man answered, "To keep the elephants away." The passer-by stated in indignation, "There aren't any elephants in New York!" Whereupon the gesturer said proudly, "See—it works!"

So—take my advice and *be careful*, because then, like the gesturer, you can assume that you remain safe because your prevention campaign works!

How do I begin dating again?
Simply by saying yes when a nice guy asks you out.

Remember the articles you used to read in *Seventeen* magazine about how to be a good date? They're still valid, but tempered with your maturity and experience. You are no longer an awkward, callow girl, but a desirable, experienced woman, which is even more fascinating.

From the first, send out messages that say you are a

thoughtful, caring woman by asking if he prefers to meet somewhere or to pick you up (keeping in mind my earlier admonitions). Don't recoil in horror at this suggestion! You don't need him to prove that you are respected as a woman by fetching you—*you* know your self-worth. What you are is a kind, considerate, mature woman who realizes that he may have a late meeting, live very far away, or have little time to rush home and change—and you want to make his life easy and comfortable from the start.

In this chapter I include the comments of several men I interviewed for the man's point of view about dating. Some of them married late and had dated hundreds of women. For simplicity's sake, I'll call them all "Stan" and "Jim."

(Jim: "Be ready on time. It's awkward to have to sit around chatting with your roommate, children, or parents when you don't know them." Stan: "It wasn't a problem for me. I always telephoned about an hour before, and asked how she was running. We would adjust the time then, if necessary for either of us.")

Greet him with a kiss on the cheek. A man always appreciates this. He may also feel a little awkward on his first date with you, and find it reassuring to be greeted warmly. A little human contact helps break the ice. (This is not a passionately purple kiss; it's a light, ladylike kiss, such as you use when you greet your great-aunt Agatha.)

Look good! I hate to restate the obvious, but no matter how rushed you are, shower and put on fresh makeup and perfume. As I said in Chapter Two, your clothes must be pressed and clean and your grooming impeccable. If you want to attract a nice man or a worldly man who will take you to interesting places, you have to be someone he's proud to have on his arm. If he hasn't told you where you're going, play it safe with the previously discussed blouse-and-skirt ensemble (maybe adding a pretty blazer), or wear a conservative dress. If you are overdressed, you

will feel awkward. Underdressing can always be interpret-
ed as conservative and ladylike. (Jim: "No one *dislikes* conservative clothes." Stan: "Women should realize that if
they're attractive, they don't have to wear revealing
clothes. It doesn't add to their beauty to wear wild plunging necklines that reveal their breasts, or dresses with slits
up to the thigh. It just isn't necessary.")

Wear something soft. I learned that men love the feel
of a soft fabric when they take your arm or put their arm
around you. They may not even be aware of it, but at some
subliminal level it appeals to their sensuality. Think about
it—would you like to touch itchy, hard fabrics? Wear soft
wools or knits, silky fabrics or velvets when possible.

If he asks you what you would like to do, hesitate first
and ask if he has made any plans. (Stan: "If you ask the
woman, it is hard for her to decide at the last minute. It's
better for the man to make some sort of plan for the date.")
If he has, try to go along with his plans unless they include
a drug drop in the woods or something similarly antisocial.
After you know each other better, you can also take the lead
with plans.

Be a good sport. Do things sometimes that you may
not feel like doing, and he will do the same for you. For instance, one of my dates "schlepped" to a fashion show
with me, and I went fishing with him—things we were
equally unenthusiastic about. What really counts is the
time you're spending together. Of course, as Jim says, "I
don't think a woman should ever go along with something
she absolutely hates. It isn't fair to the man, who wants her
to have a good time. If he wants to take her to a stock-car
race and she would abhor it, she should speak up and not
suffer all evening."

Be a good listener. By listening carefully you can draw
him out conversationally, get to know him, and have fun.
Cultivate the art of active listening, which involves reflect-

ing back someone else's statements in order to clarify what
was said: For example:

DUMB

HE: "Last week I had to go to Chicago on business,
and for the first time the weather was decent."

YOU: "Is the weather usually awful in Chicago?"

HE: "Of course. Don't you know the old joke? If you
don't like the weather in Chicago, just wait twenty minutes
and it will change."

YOU: "No. I never heard it—but I sure won't forget it
now!"

By clarifying his statement, you can get the conversation
moving. Here's another example:

HE: "Did you see the *Today* show this morning? While
I was getting dressed I happened to see Gene Shalit pan-
ning that new movie at the Rialto. He was so funny."

YOU: "He panned it? What was it he said?"

You see, there's nothing earth-shaking about active listening. It just helps the conversation flow along. You also get
more than yes and no answers with this kind of feedback.
    Try not to seem as if you are prying into his personal af-
fairs. Wait until he's willing to tell you or until the subject
comes up naturally. As for *your* personal affairs, remember:
*don't talk about the other men you have or had in your life, or about
your former husband.* (Jim: "I hated it when women told me
about their other dates and where they had taken them,
and what they did.") If he asks about your former husband,
be brief, and do not talk bitterly about him even if you have
those feelings. It is extremely unbecoming to do so. Also,
it's a bore and a turn-off for a man to listen to a woman ex-

pound on what a dog her ex is or what an angel her dear departed was. Harping on your ex makes you seem . . . well,
bitter, and like a harpy. Besides, your date will think you
might talk about him the same way you discuss your previous men, and that will frighten him away. If he thinks
your departed husband was a saint, he will feel that he
can't compete with your memories, and may back off. A
good reply for a divorcee might be, "We were married for
ten years and things just didn't work out. We're both happier now." For a widow: "I had a good marriage with John,
but I'm ready now to start a new life."

Do _not_ discuss the state of your health, and only mention your children if asked. Then, be as brief as possible.
(Jim: "Don't drag out the wallet with ten pictures of the
children or grandchildren before you even get out the
door.") Remember, you want to be seen as a possible _love
object._ This is your goal at all times, and don't forget it! At
first, it is hard for a man to see a "mommy," a grandma, a
sickly woman, or a bitter rejected woman as a romantic figure—so it's smart to downplay these roles until the romance is well established.

What do men like in a woman?

Men like feminine, sweet women! How do I know? They have
told me so. Even if you run a corporation by day, shed your
corporate skin on a date. No matter what men say or how
they act, their basic wish is for a loving someone to take care
of them and to nurture them. The same is true for most
women. (It's related to a wish for the unconditional love we
received as infants.) I once heard a panel of so-called eligible bachelors vent their frustrations and disappointment
with today's women. Their main complaint was that they
couldn't find women who wanted to take care of them at
home and tend to their needs.

One front-page article in the _Wall Street Journal_

cf.
Fromm on
Freud

(January 25, 1984) announced, "American Men Find Asian Brides Fill the Unliberated Bill." The article discusses the fifty competing services that provide American men with introductions by mail to Asian women. A professor from the University of Texas at Tyler estimates that American men currently seeking Asian wives number "in the tens of thousands," and that the trend cuts across all socioeconomic groups. Most of them express disillusionment with the liberated American woman. In 1982, 6,059 visas were issued to Asian, Latin American, and European women to come to this country to marry American men. That means 6,059 fewer men for American women to marry. You may agree with the statement in the *Journal* article that these men haven't got what it takes to compete for American women; that they are only looking for a maid and a mistress and taking advantage of poor women who want to upgrade themselves. Possibly true. But it *is* an indicator of how some of the men in this country are thinking.

A brilliant, successful, well-known beauty who married a wealthy, powerful tycoon the second time around once said, "To the outside world, a man's home is his castle—but to those on the inside, it is his nursery." I feel that if you love a man or care about him, you want to take care of him within the limits of your time. I enjoyed nurturing and helping the men I loved and am now doing this for my number-one love, my husband.

If a man is worth his salt, he will reciprocate. If not, you wouldn't want him anyhow—nurturing should be a two-way street. And isn't this what it's really all about—two people caring about and for each other? In the second century B.C., the philosopher Hecato stated: "I will show you a love potion without drug or herb or any witch's spell; if you wish to be loved, love."

"Men turn to women for the warmth and empathy they don't often find in fellowship with other men," it is stated in *Singles*. So send out little messages from the beginning that you're different from him—you, my dear, are a *woman*, with all the wonderful differences that men love and want. Keep this in mind first and foremost. When in doubt about how to react, think about what will make him feel good, not what will satisfy your need for power or control. When he feels good, he will love you. (Of course, there are limits to this; I don't expect you to be a doormat!)

Two women who run a matrimonial bureau in England asked the men who came to their office what they liked in women, and the men enumerated the following qualities: not bossy, opinionated, or argumentative; gentle and sweet but not spineless; soft voice; good listener; laughs easily; kind; good-natured; shows that she likes him; shows pleasure at his attentions; shares his interests; not bored or pessimistic or alarmist; not indifferent or hard; affectionate; intelligent; has common sense. Tall order—no?? But you can see the basic thread running through most men's requirements for a woman they can love—it is gentleness and kindness.

Back to basics. Always be a lady. Don't be coarse or swear, even if you're in a group where other women are doing it. When you're with one man, don't flirt with or stare at other men, no matter how tempting. Unfortunately, most men feel at some level that all women are potential harlots anyway. There's no need to reinforce that image. (Jim: "How did you know that?") Always try to make him feel that you're holding your sexuality in reserve for him alone, and only he has the power to unleash the passion brewing beneath your lady-like exterior. (Remember the example of the late, lovely Grace Kelly. She always appeared cool and composed on the surface but inevitably had passionate, fiery love scenes in her films.)

Be affectionate. Hold his arm at times and kiss his cheek at the dinner table if you feel like it, *but don't be phony*. The feelings should be genuine. Men like affectionate women, even if they themselves are rigid and staid. <u>"Restraint" is the key word here.</u> Don't wrap yourself around him in public, clinging like a snake, and say that *I* said to do it! Remember, you are a *lady*, but a lady who can feel warmth and affection. If you let your natural feminine feelings come through instead of repressing them because someone has told you that men are the enemy, these actions will be natural and not "put on." I know few women who don't enjoy letting this side of themselves show. We are traditionally the sex that is comfortable with stroking a fevered brow, rubbing a sore back, nursing a hurt kitten, and tenderly caring for our young, and that is the part of us our men want to see. <u>They need it desperately.</u>

<u>Be conscious of your voice.</u> A soft, modulated voice connotes sensuality, calm, and poise. Shrill laughter and a loud harsh rasp are unattractive. No screaming or shouting allowed unless you're at the prizefights or football game, or being attacked by muggers.

Working on the sound of my voice is the easy part—it's the conversational voids I'm worried about. You say I should be wary of talking about the kids, my health, my ex—what's left?
If you're working, you can always tell anecdotes or people stories. You can talk about your travels, your childhood and your parents (within limits), your school years, your profession, your siblings, the latest news stories, movies you've seen, books you've read, sports that interest you, and your philosophy of life.

Talk about *him*. Be genuinely interested. But—and this is a big "but"—don't talk too much. Incessant chatter is boring, and many women do chatter when they're nervous. <u>Unless he is very quiet, try to follow his conversational lead. I also don't believe in telling *all*.</u> Leave something unknown and mysterious. (Jim: "A woman should be a little reserved or shy and not tell the story of her life right away.") Let him wonder about your past loves or who else you may be seeing now. He doesn't have to know that you haven't had a date in six months! Why would you tell him that? Think of yourself as an onion, with layers of your personality to be peeled away over time. If he asks you a question that you don't want to answer, you can always look demure and say, "When I know you better, I'll be able to talk about that with you—right now, it would make me uncomfortable. Do you mind?" (If he does, he's a cad.)

If you speak on the telephone frequently, don't tell him everything you do on the nights that you don't see each other. Imply that you're leading an interesting life, but that you're always delighted to hear from *him*. Men can forgive most things if you're interesting. You can even be a little kookie—as long as you aren't dull. (Stan: "The reason most men don't call back after a date is that there is no chemistry.") According to the experts, the leading cause of a man's loss of interest in a woman is a vapid, dull personality. He drops her not because she's bad in bed, unattractive, or lacking wealth—but because she's boring. So take heed of Mother Rusty's advice and BE INTERESTING, DARN IT!

I've gotten through my first date with a new man, and I've had a wonderful time! He's escorted me to my door . . . now what do I do?
When you say good night after a first date, it can be awkward. If you don't invite him in he may think that you don't like him, and if you do, he may take it as an invitation to bed down with you. You just have to judge each circumstance individually. (Stan: "Inviting a man in is a way of saying, 'I enjoyed the evening and don't want it to end.' ") If you don't want to invite him in, however, just smile sweetly, kiss him on the cheek, and use an early meeting or tennis

game as an excuse for not being able to linger with him. If you like him a lot, use your instincts about whether or not the date should end at the door. (If *he* seems anxious to leave, your problem is solved, of course.) Don't forget to tell him how much you enjoyed his company, if you did. That will be his cue to say, "Can I see you again?" Or you can take the initiative and invite *him* to something. "My friend, Joan," you might say, "is having a little get-together next week for the Fourth of July. If you're not busy, would you like to come?"

To bed or not to bed is always a knotty problem. You'll have to follow your best judgment. There are no hard and fast rules, and you never know whether you're doing the right thing. It's sort of a lose-lose proposition. If you find him devastatingly attractive and irresistible, you'll have trouble saying no just because you think it's too soon. If he has been very kind, caring, and considerate all evening and has entertained you royally, you'll feel a certain obligation toward him. Of course, you aren't really indebted, but sometimes the feeling is there anyhow. When you combine that with advances on his part, there's the old dilemma again. (Which is one reason some women prefer to pay for themselves on a date—no obligation.) Try to keep in mind that single men enjoy having good company for dinner, and they are not doing *you* a favor by feeding you. (Stan: "Men don't like women who are 'pincushions.' The minute you get in the door they're taking off their clothes. He'll have no respect for you.")

If he has been obnoxious and comes on strong, then you'll feel no ambivalence about saying "no"—but you still have to be tactful. I hate to say this, but some men are capable of becoming ugly and violent if their attentions are refused. This is a reason to avoid secluded situations until you know him well. If you are afraid, you can always be evasive until you arrive at some place that is safer. For instance, if he parks the car and starts to make unwanted advances, lead him to believe that you want to wait till you're home before you settle into a little romance with him. At your door, where presumably there is someone in the house, the light is brightly lit, or the doorman is standing guard, you can peck him on the cheek and dash inside before he knows what hit him. You hope you screened out the crazies beforehand, but you can't always know. This is another reason to meet a man at a restaurant or bar or other place on the first date rather than have him pick you up.

Back to the man you feel loving toward. After a while, I found that going to bed with a man too soon ("too soon" being a subjective thing) was bound to be a negative experience. It's hard to engage in the most intimate of behavior with a virtual stranger. On the other hand, you may be in one of your "deprived" periods and want to trade your convictions for some closeness and touching (see Chapter Four).

You're bound to make some mistakes in judgment along the way. You may feel rotten if you go to bed with him and he never calls you again. But if you went to bed for the right reasons, it can be OK. The right reason to go to bed with him is to fulfill your needs, and then there won't be any self-recriminations or regrets. _You_ and _your_ needs at the moment are important here, not what you think _he_ wants. A wrong reason to go to bed with him is as a manipulative technique for "snaring" him or endearing yourself to him—you will inevitably be disappointed. By following this rule, I think you'll generally make good decisions. You still may "lose" a guy you wanted because your needs and his did not mesh that time, but he probably would have "dropped" you anyhow. When a man and a woman have good chemistry and really like each other, no harm is likely to be done by either going to bed or not going to bed.

By the way, a number of today's men complain that

women expect sex all the time, and they are so tired of having to perform that they actually take a break from dating
for a while. Meanwhile, women still believe that it's *men*
who want sex all the time. Try to remember that they don't.
One older man I know recently married a woman his own
age. He said he got tired of young things wanting sex after
they had gone out for dinner and the evening. At the end of
a big meal with some drinks, when he was tired and full, he
didn't feel like performing. Their demands got to be too
much for him, and he settled down with a nice mature lady
who understood that sex was better for older men in the
morning.

Should I call him after our date?
This is the time for another one of Rusty's Axioms. After
one date, *never* call a man who doesn't call you, no matter
what the *other* books say. Men can holler from now to tomorrow that they're flattered when women call them, but I
say, "Remember, there is no man, anywhere, at any time,
in any circumstance, who can't get in touch with a woman
if he wants to. If he doesn't want to, all the phone calls from
you won't make one whit of difference." (Stan and Jim
agree.) You can justify it by thinking that maybe he's shy,
maybe he thought you didn't like him, maybe he lost your
telephone number, maybe he's busy at work, maybe he had
to go out of town . . . you fill in the blanks. Save yourself
some heartache. Whatever they say, men still like to do the
pursuing. (Stan and Jim: "True.")
    After he has shown some interest and pursued a bit,
then you can call back and forth. But not until then. Otherwise he will always remember that it was you who called
him, and the gal who looks a little unattainable will appeal
to him more.
    I called a man *once*, early in my single life. It only em-
barrassed both of us. He was forced to come up with some
ridiculous statement about calling me when he came back

from Europe in six weeks. He couldn't call me before that because he was leaving in *two weeks.* Needless to say, I never heard from him—and I felt stupid. I also learned a valuable lesson, which I am passing on to you. Don't even be *tempted* to call him after a first date!

After he calls you for another date, and then for a third, a fourth, and so on, you can be pretty sure that a relationship is in the making. Now you can start feeling freer to call him, to invite him to do things, to introduce him to your friends and family, to include him in some of your plans for holidays and vacations. You'll know when things are moving along. If your loving feelings are emerging and you decide that you would like to marry this man, now is the time to become so much a part of his life that he will get used to you and your loving ways, and will want you near always.

This is not to say that you can't drop hints to a man that you'd like to go out with him the *first* time. If you see a man frequently at work or play, for instance, you can always say something like, "I'd like to know you better. Why don't you give me a call sometime?" or "I'm going roller skating next week with So-and-so. Maybe you'd like to come along." After that, though, it's up to him. The ball in in his court.

What if he ends the evening with that infamous male line (or lie) "I'll call you tomorrow (or Monday, or next week, or when I get back from Kansas City)"? *Don't wait around for that call*—most of the time it never comes. Erica Abeel, in her book *I'll Call You Tomorrow, And Other Lies Men Tell Women,* theorizes that this is an example of "man-speak," a different language that women must learn. When a man says, "I'll call you," she states, he is merely trying to be gracious when he takes leave of you after an evening. He may also regard this statement as a sort of raincheck he can cash in months later, or as a way of avoiding hassles. Abeel thinks women should try to break the code: "Let's elope to Brazil" should be understood with the amendment, "if something else doesn't come up"!

POSTSCRIPT: Dating can be complex these days and hazardous to your finances! The *New York Times* of July 26, 1978, carried a story with the headline "Jilted California Accountant Sues His Date for $38 in Expenses." He felt that his date did not "make a 'good faith effort' to inform him that she was canceling their date for dinner and the theater before he drove to San Francisco from San Jose, 50 miles to the south." The plaintiff explained that the lady had two weeks to call him before the date. He computed his costs at 17 cents a mile for the 100-mile trip, two hours of his time at his minimum rate of $8.50 an hour, and court costs. The defendant told the judge that she canceled the date at the last minute because she had to work late. The plaintiff, however, said that he brought suit because "there's too much of this thing, broken dates."

Forewarned is forearmed!

To recap Mother Rusty's Tips for Happy Dating:

1. Don't worry about botching it at first—you may and it's OK.

2. Offer to meet him somewhere if he wishes.

3. Greet him with a kiss.

4. Look good.

5. Be ready on time.

6. Go along with his plans unless they're absolutely abhorrent to you.

7. Be a good listener.

8. Do not discuss your health, your ex, or your children unless asked, and then make it brief.

9. Be warm, nurturing, and womanly.

10. Be a lady.

11. Be affectionate.

12. Be soft-spoken.

13. Be interesting.

14. Don't tell all.

15. After one or two dates, if you don't hear from him, don't call him.

16. Use your best judgment about inviting him in and/or bedding down.

17. Only go to bed with him to fill *your* needs at the time, whether for sex or for closeness. Do not go to bed with him as a means of endearing yourself to him.

I'm a single mother. Could you talk about some of the special problems I might have with dating?
Dating when you have children does present special problems, but most can be handled with some additional planning. Twenty percent of all children in the United States under the age of eighteen (or 12,512,000) are living only with their mothers. This represents an increase of 67,000 children between 1982 and 1983. Most men have no qualms about dating you, as it's a fact of today's life that many single women are mothers.

You, however, may have some concerns. Even the logistics of leaving the house for a date can be a major problem for the single mother. Usually she is very busy, holds down a job, does household chores, helps the children with their homework, and tries to make ends meet. Many simply choose not to date for a while, as they just can't cope with the realities of getting out for an evening. A date only takes away from time spent with their children, and it competes for the time they need for themselves. They must also spend money on baby sitters or clothes, which could be used for other essentials. If a date goes badly, it can be very frustrating and disappointing to make these sacrifices.

Yet most women agree that they need the lift that dating provides. They find that when they do something fun for themselves, they can face their responsibilities better. They need to be given to instead of always giving. Herein lies the dilemma.

As usual, it is the woman who has to juggle her life to try to enjoy a normal existence. If you are a widow, needless to say, you bear full responsibility for your children and your life. If you're divorced, your ex usually does not have custody of the children and can come and go as he pleases, or even live with someone. But he'll be quick to object to *your* dating. He won't want you to bring men home to meet "his" children. You may also worry about gossip from the neighbors if they see men coming and going. In fact, the very same people who urge the single mother to get out of the house and find someone may turn around and criticize her for neglecting her children if she becomes involved with a man. Add to all this the objections of the children themselves, especially during two sensitive periods in their development; five to seven years old or in early adolescence, and you have a real stew. Kids can be very jealous of your dates or boyfriends, and make your life miserable. Most people agree that you just have to wait out these periods and live your life as normally as possible. You can't let the children interfere with your right to live a complete life. They must not be allowed to bully you.

Then there's the issue of sex and how you handle it. Some women don't want their children to see them as having sexual needs or as a sexual person. Others feel it is a normal and natural part of life that their children must learn to accept. Opinions differ, even among the experts, but Dr. Ann Ruben, a family and child therapist, states in

Singles that it isn't wise to base your relationships on a child's sanctions. It gives the child too much power. But she also states that a single parent must act as a proper role model if she expects or demands appropriate sexual behavior from her children. She encourages women *not* to sleep with men when children are in the house, and stresses that single parents "must keep their sexual relationships separate from their children." She encourages them to "use a motel or go to an apartment where they will have privacy . . . especially so that the children don't see them in bed together. What a single parent does sexually is privileged information. I don't think they ought to disclose it to their children at any age."

In reality, of course, many women handle it differently. They may not have the luxury of another place for sex, so they try to have the man leave early before children or neighbors are awake. This can backfire if a child awakens during the night and comes into your room, and can cause some problems. You will simply have to work this out according to your children's ages, your comfort zone, the limits on your time, and your living arrangements.

Men also differ in their opinions about the propriety of spending the night with women who have children at home. Some will never do it; they agree with Dr. Ruben that other places are better for sex. Some don't mind, and take it for granted that they will sleep at the homes of their ladies. They accept the fact that they may have to leave before the children awaken, and cooperate gladly. Other men feel that it is "cheap" for a woman to allow this. (Stan thinks so.) Some men are insensitive and don't even understand what all the fuss is about.

People also have different ways of handling the issue of who pays the baby sitter. Some consider it part of the dating expense, and the man pays the sitter and his or her cabfare, if necessary. (Stan: "This is what I always did." Jim: "I never did.") Others consider it the mother's responsibility, and she handles the expense. It's an individual issue.

Since 43% of single mothers and 42% of single fathers wish to remarry, some satisfactory arrangements must be worked out. Here are a few suggestions:

1. Talk to your kids. Explain to the younger ones that you need a life of your own. They mustn't think they can take the place of a grown-up relationship in your life. Discuss your needs with your older children. They will sometimes be jealous, and you will have to expect that. But let them know that you're happier when you date, and tell them how important it is to you. Try to downplay your involvement with a man only if it is affecting them seriously. If it is, you may want to meet your date on more neutral ground for a time. Adolescents can be obnoxious and embarrass you in front of your dates. They can insult them, call them by the names of other men, drop comments about other men in your life (even if there are none), or drop hints about wanting you to get married, and who needs that?

2. When you are initially dating someone, get him out of the house fairly quickly. It's silly to expect every man you meet to form a relationship with your kids. Try to bring them together only as you become more serious with someone. Use the "need to know" principle. Don't tell your kids anything that they don't "need to know" until it is necessary—and they don't "need to know" every man that you date.

3. You don't owe your ex-husband explanations for your dating behavior. Shut off his attempts at inter-

ference firmly and politely. You don't have to justify what you are doing as long as you feel that you're acting responsibly. He no longer has a say in your life unless you allow it.

4. Keep displays of affection to a minimum in front of the children. You can do your lovey-dovey thing in private—flaunting your sensuality only creates problems. Children may be very ambivalent about their father's absence from the home, and may become very angry at your affection for a replacement. No need to inflame that.

5. Let the children have more responsibility for themselves and the household. Unless children are very young, they don't need constant tending like little seedlings. Some expectations for their independence go a long way toward making kids and parents happier. Your house and children don't have to be perfect. Let them help, and allow them to develop their autonomy. It leads to greater self-esteem for them—and more fun time for you!

6. Call on grandparents and relatives to help (if they're willing, of course!). Let the children spend time with family in order to give you time alone for travel, romance, or rest. The grandparents may be delighted, and everyone will be happier.

7. Investigate Parents Without Partners or similar support groups. There you will meet others in similar situations and you can exchange ideas, meet people, and participate in the social events they sponsor that include children.

I'm sure you'll come up with some creative solutions of your own. It *is* possible to be a good mother and still have

time for yourself, but you may have to make some accom-
modations, such as dating later in the evening or juggling
things a little. It's important though, to move into dating
slowly, so that the children have a chance to get used to the
idea. It's another big adjustment for the child who has already had to adjust to many changes in his or her life. Also,
you can't date every night, as you do need to be there for
your family. But with a little ingenuity, planning, energy,
and intelligence you *can* date and have satisfactory relationships with men. We women have traditionally risen to challenges, right?

Good luck, and have a good time!

CHAPTER SIX

The Right Man for You

Now that you're dating, it's time for you to sit down and do some thinking about the kind of husband you're looking for. If you followed my outline in Chapter One and reflected on what went wrong with your marriage and what you liked or disliked about your previous husband, you're already off to a good start. You know what worked and what didn't work for you in the past. Now consider the *new* you you've become, and be completely honest about your needs. If you know that you want a husband with money, for instance, go ahead and admit it! No one else is going to know except you. If a habit of your other spouse used to drive you crazy, it's OK to want a man who won't repeat that behavior.

While you define your expectations, though, it's important not to get caught up in the clichés of our times. *You* may prefer qualities that seem old-fashioned or out of step with those desired by many of today's women, and that's all right. Your goal is to be happy when you remarry, and hopefully you've learned some things about yourself and marriage that will keep you from repeating the sad history you left behind.

What should I look for in a second mate?
In general, people's expectations are more realistic the second time around. They are looking for a friend rather than a great love. Nevertheless, *you* may have some needs that are very specific. If you have young children, for instance, you'll no doubt look for someone who will be a good parent to them. If you're immersed in your career, you will need a man who understands your commitment and won't be jealous or possessive about the time you devote to it. If you want a traditional life, where the wife stays home and the man supports the family, your man will have to hold the same values or trouble will lie down the road. If you feel the pressure of your biological time clock ticking away and want children, your mate must share your ideas about having a family. If *he* has children, you must be reasonably sure you can tolerate them. The important thing is to figure out what *you* need to be happy, and then to find someone who can meet these needs.

But doesn't that sound selfish?
Yes, but it's the right kind of selfishness. You're only being honest and self-aware. You *have* to be if you want a good relationship—one in which you are free to be your best nurturing, giving, loving self for your mate because you know your needs will also be satisfied. This can happen only if you choose your man carefully.

I asked some remarried women for their definition of a "good man." Here are some of their replies:

- "He's understanding, considerate, loving, honest, open, believes in God."

- "A good man is one who is generous, considerate, loving, willing to work things out, understanding, unselfish, and helpful."

- "One who is just, compassionate, and fair—one who accepts a commitment."

- "Someone who meets your expectations and can enhance your life, someone who is nurturing, loving, and supportive."

- "He's kind, generous, not macho, understanding toward my children and family—we have compatible interests."

- "Someone who can meet my emotional needs and is sensitive."

As you can see, certain themes recur: a good man is loving, understanding, emotionally open, and able to commit to a relationship. Yet these are difficult qualities to find in men. They could be classified as the more "feminine" qualities, which women have traditionally valued and learned and which they express in their relationships with men and women alike. Men are more likely to value strength, competitiveness, responsibility, and carefully contained emotion, simply because they have been socialized to do so from birth. Studies have shown that more demands are made upon boys from the beginning, and that they learn to cope with life differently from girls.

Does this mean I have to settle for the "strong, silent type"?

Not necessarily. If you meet a man who happens to be sharing, caring, empathetic, sensitive, emotionally open, and able to cry, that's great, but he doesn't *have* to be those things to be a satisfactory life partner, lover, or friend. You can still share intimate thoughts, feelings, and confidences with your women friends. After all, you're looking for a husband, not a substitute girlfriend!

The women quoted above did not find *all* those qualities in the men they eventually married, but they are happily wed anyhow. Personally *I* appreciate many things about
the traditional man—the one who doesn't cry easily or who
is uncomfortable looking weak—as long as he also believes
that he should meet his responsibilities and take care of his
wife and children. He usually feels that he should be strong
and protective, and he's competitive and somewhat aggressive. He may not share his feelings easily, but he can
listen to you and offer his support and encouragement. He
is *dependable*. You can be sure that he will be there for you
when you are ill, say, even if he can't admit that it frightens
him when you're sick. So, don't discount this type of man.

How will I know what he's really like?
You can sometimes tell after one conversation, date, or
phone call. Remember that most people telegraph what
they're like. Don't invest time with a man who doesn't suit
you because you think you can change him. If a man tells
you something about himself, believe him! Don't fall into
this kind of wishful thinking:

HE: "I've never been able to stand kids. They're all rug
rats to me."

SHE: (to herself): "Wait till he gets to know mine. He'll
love them."

I think that some of women's cynical and negative feelings
toward men stem from the fact that they set themselves up
for disappointment. Don't let your eagerness for a relationship blind you to the truth. When you meet a man, *read*
him. Pay attention to what he says and does. Watch how he
treats people. Does he come on to your girlfriends, fly into
rages, or bully people in menial jobs? If this man consistently disappoints you after you've spent time together, don't

invest months with him. *He* is letting you know who he is, while *you* may be trying to read something into him that just isn't there. Then you may wind up despairing that men aren't kind or gentle or attentive, when really only *this* man is not those things. If you want qualities that he doesn't possess, *move on.* Women our age don't have months or years to waste on relationships that have no prospect for being permanent (although we should and do have ancillary men in our lives). *You* know what you like, need, and want in a husband, so don't dwell on the shortcomings of men. Find one man who meets most of your needs and work with *him.*

But can't people change?
You must remember two ironclad rules:

1. No one changes his basic character permanently. This is worth repeating: NO ONE CHANGES PERMANENTLY. Even with an in-depth psychoanalysis of many years' duration, change is difficult to achieve.

2. Anything that upsets you about a person before marriage will *always* get worse after marriage. Remember, courtship is when people are on their best behavior!

Be sure you can tolerate everything about a man before you even consider marrying him. You can't expect him to be perfect, but be sure his flaws won't drive you crazy. I have formulated what I call Rusty's Law. It is simply this: EVERY MAN HAS A TRAGIC FLAW. Even the most adorable of male creatures will have some annoying or imperfect trait that you will have to put up with. (Men say the same thing about us, but this book is about *them.*) Some examples are:

Thoughtlessness

Impotence

Poor personal hygiene

Cheapness

Poor job record

Lack of money

Poor taste in clothes

Laziness

Tendency to abuse alcohol or drugs

Dullness

Obesity

Boorishness

Sloppiness

Awful family

Homeliness

Obnoxious children

And so on. Your problem is deciding which of these traits you can tolerate in a man who's otherwise perfect for you. For instance, if he is loving, cuddly, romantic and sexy, likes your children, takes you out to nice places, and has a nice income, but is personally sloppy and doesn't shave or bathe often enough—can you stand this? Remember, he won't change! Oh, he may change long enough for you to marry him, but he will inevitably slip back into his old habits. Or maybe he's loving, generous, attentive, and rich, but impotent for some physical or psychological reason; can you survive on cuddling, hugging, and maybe oral sex?

Or is he intelligent, aware, interesting, attentive, and a good lover, but drinks too much four nights a week, falls asleep, and doesn't remember the next morning what you talked about? Or is he handsome, loving, thoughtful, and devoted, but changes jobs every three months and never has any money? I could go on and on, but you get the idea. We all have our individual likes and dislikes, and the important thing is to know yourself well enough to know what you can tolerate *for the long term.* Once you have decided this, knowing that your man won't change, you can concentrate on getting him to march down the aisle with you.

What were you *looking for?*
My own list of qualities for my future mate included the following. I wanted him to be:

Consistent

Not moody

An "up" personality

Gregarious

Interested in doing things

Compassionate

Someone who shared my values

Sensual

Generous (not cheap)

Not a womanizer or a flirt

Someone I could talk to

Fairly well-off financially

Not controlling

Healthy

Educated and aware

Someone with hobbies

Affectionate

Intelligent

Witty and zany and fun-loving

Fond of good food and entertaining

Clean

Close to my age

Friendly to my children

Not an alcohol or drug abuser

Interesting

Sound impossible? Well, I found a man with all these marvelous qualities. Your list will be different. You may want an athlete, or an art lover, or a hunk, or a guy who loves sailing, or someone quiet . . . the list can be endless.

But aren't there also some men who will never be good marriage prospects?
Yes. Now that I've discussed what constitutes the "good man" and concluded that it can be different for each individual woman, I must also warn you that some qualities indicate a bad or inappropriate choice for a marriage partner. Some of these qualities could fit into the "tragic flaw" category; others are more serious and definite no-no's for anyone looking for a happy remarriage. Pay attention to the following list. Keep a sharp eye out for these kinds of men,

noting that one man can fit into several categories.

The M.C.P. (Male Chauvinist Pig): This guy won't let you develop your own individuality, and will try to keep you in the kitchen and the bedroom where you "belong." He will insist that your whole life revolve around him and his needs. Since you are "only a woman" he will automatically think your ideas are unimportant, and will put you down at every opportunity. You want to take care of and nurture your mate, but you also want him to regard you as an effective, accomplished human being and acknowledge the fact that you have a mind and life of your own.

The Tin Man: Need closeness and intimacy? This is not your candidate. He must be in control at all times, and if anyone gets too close, she will bang up against a sheet of cold metal. These are fine qualities for a tightrope walker or a character in a story, but in real life you want a husband with a heart.

Mr. Fixed: This creature can't tolerate any change or growth in you. Should you develop any new ideas or change your thinking one iota after you're married, he will fight you to the death. He isn't secure unless everything stays exactly the same until you meet the Grim Reaper.

The Golden Gloves Kid: Like to fight? Like to fuss? Like a good resounding argument? The Kid is never happier than when fighting or arguing. You know, the old black-is-white-if-he-says-so type. Unless you want your marriage to resemble the championship bout of the year minus Howard Cosell, beware of The Kid!

Mommy's Little Darling: You know the type. He calls his mother six times a day, and practically never goes to the

bathroom without reporting in. Mommy will be very involved in your lives, and her approval will be necessary for
every decision you make. This man will make your life miserable by constantly comparing you to her—and you'll never quite measure up. *She* will make your life miserable because she considers you a rival. What she'd really like is to
marry Sonny herself, if only it were possible.

The Always Swinging Single (A.S.S.): This creature will want
to pursue group sex, swinging, threesomes, foursomes,
worldsomes, and more, even after marriage. He will live
the same life he lived before he married you, but now he
has you at home to watch his kiddies, clean his house, earn
his living, or whatever. He will warn you before you marry
that he loves to swing, but you probably won't believe it because right now you are the object of his full attentions. He
isn't the same as the philanderer because he would love to
include you in his activities at the latest club or sex resort. If
that's not your cup of tea, *run!*

The Man Who Worships Women: He puts you on a pedestal.
He thinks women are the better sex, noble, chaste, and
pure. All this can be flattering, but you are bound to fall off
your perch one day, and then the sounds you hear will be
your marriage cracking up.

The Sexually Problematic Man: This can include a man with
whom you are blatantly incompatible sexually, someone
with an extremely low or nonexistent sexual drive, someone you suspect of being a homosexual, or someone with
kinky and exotic sexual needs that are repugnant to you.
(This can include someone who likes to dress up in your
clothes—which can be very upsetting, particularly if he
looks better in them than you do.) You may think it's un-
likely that you'd get as far as the altar with someone like

this, but men can conceal things very artfully. He may claim that he wants to wait for sex until marriage, or say he hasn't been feeling sexual lately because of some problem he is having with his boss, his tooth, his stomach, or the state of the economy. For those of us who have been married before, there are few reasons for not exploring sex with our potential mate. I urge you somehow to overcome your prohibitions and have some sexual experience with your man. If it's utterly impossible for you to do so because of strong beliefs, religious or otherwise, at least *talk* to him about sex and his feelings about it in some detail. I have never believed the old cliché that divorce begins in the bedroom, but a serious sexual problem *can* be a catalyst for the end of a marriage.

The D. & B. Man: I don't mean Dun and Bradstreet, I mean drugs and booze. Alcohol is a depressant drug. There can be a very fine line between what is considered normal drinking and what constitutes problem drinking or alcoholism. When I worked as the director of the Dade County Outpatient Center for Alcoholism Treatment, we used the following definition for the alcoholic. "An alcoholic is someone for whom alcohol presents a problem in some area of his life, whether social, vocational, physical, legal, marital, spiritual, emotional, or in the community." Another way of putting it would be to ask, "Does his drinking frequently or continuously interfere with his social relations, his role in the family, his job, his finances, or his health?" There is a presumed lack of control over the drinking as well. This is a necessarily broad definition, as alcoholism is a comprehensive disease.

Many alcoholics recover through their own efforts, a treatment program, AA, or a combination of these things. Experts agree, however, that the recovered alcoholic must never drink again if he wishes to maintain his sobriety.

People think that a person has to drink every day to be an alcoholic, or that he must have a drink in the morning for the shakes. Not true. He can go through periods of abstention, drink only on weekends, or even drink only once a year. The important factor is the loss of control and the consequences of the drinking. If a person drinks just once a year, but on that one occasion gets very drunk, smashes up his car, kills someone, beats his wife, or loses his job, he has a serious drinking problem. Normal drinkers do not create these kinds of consequences when they drink. For your information and help in spotting the disease, I list the following danger signals, taken from *Understanding and Counseling the Alcoholic* by Howard Clinebell, Jr.:

1. He persistently uses alcohol rather than personal resources to solve problems.

2. Alcohol holds a prominent place in his thinking and planning of activities.

3. He needs alcohol to gain social confidence or courage.

4. He spends money for alcohol that he really needs for the necessities of life.

5. He is defensive about how much or when he drinks.

6. He gulps drinks, or drinks in secret.

7. He drinks in the morning to cure a hangover or to "pep up" for the day.

8. He has blackouts (memory loss) when drinking.

9. He feels "normal" only when he has alcohol in him.

10. Drinking interferes with his health, home life, job, or social life.

11. His drinking behavior defies the drinking standards of his important social or fellowship group.

As for drugs—whether tranquilizers, marijuana, sleeping pills, heroin, cocaine, or prescription drugs—if a person abuses them, his life will be disrupted. If you are married to such a person, your life will also be chaotic. Many of the "danger signals" mentioned for alcohol also apply to drug abuse. Their effects may be subtler and harder to detect, however, as there may be no overt sign, such as the odor of alcohol.

Keep these admonitions in mind as you meet men. Look for the signs of drug and alcohol abuse. A recovered substance abuser can live a drug-free life forever and be a wonderful husband and father, but you deserve to make an informed decision before marrying.

Another kind of addiction, just as destructive, is:

The Compulsive Gambler: This man is out of control when it comes to gambling. He will sell anything, beg, borrow, and steal, and deprive his family for money to gamble with. The "big win" is always just around the corner, and even if it does come along, he will soon lose his winnings again. Life with such a man is a series of arguments and deprivations and has a poor prognosis for success unless he seeks help through Gamblers Anonymous and recovers some control over his compulsive behavior.

The Othello Syndrome, or the Pathologically Jealous Man: This man is extremely insecure and can be seriously mentally ill. Often the jealousy is the only symptom of his paranoia. At first you may be flattered by his attention, but it can be absolute hell to be married to such a person. He is paranoid about every man you speak to or he thinks you speak to, and may accuse you of all kinds of exotic sexual behavior with everyone from the delivery boy to the parson. He is suspicious about your every move, and may even want to keep you away from your own family because he wants you all to himself. As his behavior becomes more and more extreme you may become a prisoner in your own home. Look for signs of this sick behavior as you get to know your man, and run as fast as you can if you suspect that this is a problem. (Sometimes these men murder their mates because their sick minds convince them that she is a whore and deserves it.)

The Workaholic: What, you say, can be wrong with a man who works hard for his family? If what you desire in a marriage is long hours alone and lots of material comforts, you may be happy with this man. Or, if you, too, are a certifiable workaholic, this match can work. Some theorists are beginning to see workaholism in a more positive light, but if _you_ are looking for a dining companion and someone to take leisurely walks with after dinner, this is not your man. He'll still be at the office or the factory, and his work will be his mistress. Sometimes he will suspend his obsessive work habits long enough to court you, but he will soon revert to his old ways, and you will play second fiddle. This is not the worst of faults on a scale of one to ten, but it can lead to feelings of deprivation and loneliness on your part. Again, know your needs so that you avoid problems the second time around.

Bossy the Bull: Like to be controlled? Like never to have a say in decisions? Like to be pushed around? You'll love Bossy. He'll fill all your needs. He'll tell you what to do, what to wear, how to spend your money, how to fix your hair, when to mop the floor, how to run the house, who your friends should be, where you should work, how you should raise the children, how you should spend your vacation, ad nauseam. Enough said?

The Eternal Youth: This gentleman only looks grown up. He sulks, runs away from problems, wants his own way and wants it right now, and probably has temper tantrums as well. He also has no sense of responsibility about money, and he usually has none, because he either throws it away or frequently loses his job. It's always the boss's fault when he gets fired; he is always smarter than the boss, who fails to realize it.

A man like this is an expert in preying on mature women with good jobs, and invariably finds women who can support him. He is often very loving and sweet, and a woman can enjoy lots of love, attention, and good sex with him. In return he usually gets mothered, is given an allowance or "loans," and can be very hard to get rid of when you've had enough of playing surrogate mother. He's very good at crying and making you feel guilty when you try to expel him from your home, which he has cunningly managed to infiltrate. His shirts creep one by one into your closet, soon followed by his stereo, inversion boots, and all the rest of his things. If you have a maid, she is soon laundering his clothes, and you're picking up his dry cleaning.

Sometimes a very motherly woman can be happily married to this kind of man, but it is rare. In time, she usually gets fed up with his boyish charm and begins to want a grown-up man for her partner. After he leaves, you will get calls for months afterwards from the various people to whom he owes money, so be prepared.

The Hypochondriac: We all have aches and pains occasionally, but the hypochondriac thrives on them. He is constantly at the doctor's office, and usually there is nothing wrong with him. This is really just attention-getting behavior (although on an unconscious level of awareness), and can be very hard to deal with in a marriage unless you are a *very* nurturing individual who doesn't mind listening to his constant physical complaints. You may become hostile and resentful toward this man, and there goes your marriage.

The Neurotic: The man with serious neurotic problems such as severe, crippling phobias, anxiety states, manic states, or depressive cycles is a poor marital risk. He may not be functional in the world or in his work for periods of time. From time to time he may require extensive treatment, whether counseling, medication, or hospitalization. This man can be loved and looked upon with compassion, but as a marriage partner he can drain you emotionally and financially until the relationship is badly damaged and you are very unhappy. Sometimes a woman who can only feel strong and effective when her partner is needy and weak can sustain a marriage with this type of man, but usually such a marriage carries a poor prognosis for happiness.

The Sociopath: Remember Murph the Surf, a charming jewel thief in the news during the sixties? This is the prototype of a sociopathic personality—a charming scamp whose development went awry somewhere along the way, and he failed to develop a superego or conscience. He breaks the law with impunity and has no feelings of guilt or awareness of how he has hurt others. He lies pathologically, and has no sense of right or wrong. Since this man is usually very charming, you can easily be taken in by him, but if your Rusty Radar System is working, you can pick up the signals. (Lying is one of the most obvious.) BEWARE!!!

Mr. Cheapskate: There's a fine line between frugality and

plain old cheapness. This man knows many ways to squeeze a nickel, and has short arms and deep pockets. He sponges on anyone he can, and is a taker rather than a giver. As his wife, your life will not be much fun, as he will never want to spend money on "frivolous" things. Even if you have your own money, his philosophy will put a damper on the way you spend it. If you don't have a job or much money, life with this man will be hell. You will never be free to buy anything spontaneously, and he will only give you money if every cent is accounted for and justified.

The other side of the "coin," equally devastating to a marriage, is—

The Spendthrift: Mr. Extravagant is everybody's friend; Good Time Charlie takes a back seat to him. He treats everyone in sight to breakfast, lunch, dinner or drinks, lends money to anyone who asks, gives presents galore, and is the champion check grabber of the Western world. These are lovable traits unless and until they mean deprivation for you and the children. You may have to beg for household money or shoe money for the kids. You see, it isn't that he is so generous, it's that he feels he has to buy love from the world because his self-esteem is so poor.

The Bully: Although he will always be contrite afterwards, run as fast as you can from a physically abusive man. Whether or not he has been drinking, there is _never_—I repeat, _never_— an excuse for a man to hit a woman. This man will not improve after marriage, so don't ever fool yourself into thinking that all he needs to change him is a little love and affection from a good woman. He won't change, and will most likely get worse. To enter a marriage with a man like this may trap you for life, as he won't let you get away from him without fear for your life and your children's. This is serious, serious business, and I urge you strongly to beware of this man, no matter how loving he can be at other times.

The Gold Digger: I hate to be cynical, but unfortunately there are still some men who are looking for a woman with money and who will go to any length to woo and win her. Even if you aren't rich, you may have come into a sum of money from your husband's death or from a divorce settlement. When we are needy and lonely, we can be very vulnerable to charming men who are "temporarily out of funds" and just need a loan to tide them over until the big deal in Omaha is finalized. You may find that when your funds are depleted he will disappear from your life, even if you're married to him. It's a chilly world out there without bucks, and I urge you to be wary and use good common sense about a man's motives. This happened to a friend of mine after her divorce. She set up her new husband in three business ventures, which all failed. When she had no more money, he vanished.

OK. I stand forewarned and forearmed, but what happens after I find my "good man"? How do we end up married? What if I'm not madly in love with him?
Once you have found the man who fills most of your needs and whose flaws you can accept, you can start to work on your relationship. This is when you decide whether you really want to marry him. Only *you* can decide if you want him—not your children or your mother or your best friend, although they will all offer their opinions. Just listen to your inner self.

You don't have to be madly in love. Since the beginning of marriage as an institution, people have joined together in matrimony in the craziest of circumstances. The big myth is that people marry for romantic love. Wrong! We may want to believe this, but romantic love is only one of the reasons people decide to walk hand in hand down the corridor of life. Some of the *real* reasons people marry (not necessarily in order of importance) are:

For a meal ticket

To have a housekeeper, secretary, mother, or father

To say that they did

To prove something to the world

For available sex

To avoid loneliness

To please their parents

For money

For prestige

For power

To further their career

To make political or business alliances

To get even with an old lover

To get out of the parental home

To become a United States citizen

To obtain a father or mother for their children

Because they think it's their only opportunity

To have children

Because someone else loves *them*

Because of pressure from family or society

And, yes—also because they have fallen in love.

You sound cynical about love!
Not at all. The whole subject of love and marriage is rich
with legend and lore. We all know that not only married
people experience love—yet the conviction remains that
love and marriage go together like the well-known horse
and carriage! The understatement of the year may be that
the custom of marrying for love is far from universal. Remember the Rothschilds, who only married their cousins in
order to keep the fortune in the family, and all the royal
families of the world who have traditionally eschewed love
in favor of "proper" marriages. Among many societies,
love is the result of, not the reason for, marriage, and in societies where the husband and wife are economically dependent upon each other, there is much less emphasis on
love. Also, love is more significant in contemporary Western societies than in societies in other times and places.

As Cole Porter asked, "What is this thing called love?"
The great psychologist Theodore Reik explained love as a
lack or deficiency in oneself. He stated that love starts out
as an unconscious dissatisfaction with ourselves, often felt
as a discontent with life. We find a person who we think
possesses all the excellent qualities we lack and who appears to be self-sufficient and self-satisfied. When we fall in
love, we lose the dissatisfaction with ourselves and feel ful-
filled in our beloved by making that person a part of ourselves, and our feelings of dissatisfaction give way to an ex-
ultant feeling. The deeper the self-dislike, the stronger the
passion aroused by the love object. Thus, says Reik, "falling in love has the character of a rescue—it brings the person into emotional safety like bringing a drowning swim-
mer to the shore." This theory also explains the disillusionment we feel after we get to know a person and find that he
is only a flawed human being like ourselves.

Not very romantic, is it, when looked at this way?
From the perspective of maturity vs. youth, those who are

young and immature would be more likely to "fall in love" in Reik's sense, as their self-esteem may be shakier and they may have stronger feelings of discontent. The older person, who is more sure of herself or himself, may not need "rescuing" and can love for the right reasons.

In my opinion, the right reasons are expressed best by psychoanalyst Harry Stack Sullivan's definition of love. "When the satisfaction or the security of another person becomes as significant to one as one's own satisfaction or security, then the state of love exists." This definition fits most closely my idea of the kind of love one should feel for one's prospective mate. It might be called a kind of "like" instead of love, which involves a mutual caring and commitment and an acceptance of real life and its demands. You want to help this person have a happier life, and as a by-product your life will be enhanced as well.

The following comments were made by successfully remarried women about why they chose the men they did:

"I was tired of men who didn't care how I felt. I wanted someone who would just give a darn about me. In return, I was willing to give all I had to someone who would be loving with me. Jack is wonderful, and fills my emotional needs. He is uncomfortable with me when I cry, but he doesn't try to make me stop. He just holds me and lets me get it out of my system. Sometimes I wish he would take better care of himself and slow down, but I know that it is hard for him to change. We have problems, sure, but we're a team. He wasn't what you would call good-looking, but he was so nice and kind, I just felt all those loving feelings for him."

"My first husband was very moody, and you never knew what kind of reception you would get when you approached him. Everyone had to tiptoe around the house until we knew how he felt that day or that minute. My new husband is an open, cheerful guy who is always the same. I know he gets angry or tired sometimes, but he doesn't take it out on me. He lies down or goes out and hits some tennis balls. It was important for me to have a consistent man in my life."

"When I was widowed, I felt that I would never meet anyone as wonderful as my first husband. My life with him had involved lots of travel and entertaining. When I met Fred, I was suspicious because he was so involved with me from the beginning. He was so thoughtful, and always tried to think of ways to please me and the children. He was desperate for love and affection, and aroused my maternal instincts. Even though he is totally different from Joe, I felt love for him, also. I knew that I wanted to marry him when he went away on business and I missed him. My life is different now—we do outdoor things and play golf, which I never did before, but we've been married three years now and it has been very fulfilling for me."

"I was very tired of the sameness of my life when I met Leo. It was the same old thing, day in and day out. Work, home, kids, TV, dinner. Every man I met was uninterested in a woman with children; they wanted to 'swing' and 'keep their options open.' Leo wasn't afraid to show me that he cared and he didn't mind the children. Although he is not rich, and he works long hours, we are happy. Someone else might not like him because he has a pot belly and doesn't dress too well, but he is the kindest and funniest man I know. He always cheered me up, and he still does."

"I'm a lawyer and my new husband isn't. But he likes having a professional for a wife and never hassles me about the hours I spend at work. He tries to make life easier for me when he can. He won't do domestic chores or shop or cook—but he doesn't demand that I do it either. We eat out a lot and I have a cleaning woman. He has children who live with his ex-wife, and because I am busy with my career, I don't resent the time that he spends with them. When he and I are together, we're never bored, and though he has some macho qualities, I know that he is on my side, and that's what counts."

Well, you still haven't told me how to get him to marry me!
I was getting to that, although in the 1930s Dorothy Dix stated: "It has been said that there are two secrets no woman ever tells. One is her age. The other is how she won her husband."

Once you have met a man who you think has possibilities and whom you are seeing regularly, it's time to work on the relationship. The reason (and the only reason) you're seeing each other regularly is because there is chemistry and rapport between you. Remember that. Also remember that men like to be married as much as women do, if not more. As I said in Chapter One, studies show that married men are happier and healthier than single men. (They also show that *single women* are happier than single men.) They need us as much as we need them. They miss the many good things about marriage, such as having someone to go home to, having someone of their very own, the closeness at mealtimes, having someone to sleep with and share problems with, and just having someone around. These feelings usually start to reemerge within three years after becoming single, and most men remarry within three to five years.

Both of you must be finished with the experimentation phase of the years after divorce. If you don't meet a man at the proper time in both your cycles, he may not be ready when you are, or vice versa. The recently divorced man is the riskiest man. Be:ng the first or second woman in his single life is usually a losing proposition. At that point, he is still interested in experiencing the joys of being single, and he will feel that he is missing something if he settles down too soon with one woman. The same applies to you.

During the first two years or so after my divorce, I met several men who would have been very good husbands, but at that stage I wasn't ready to think about remarriage. In fact, the thought of being married depressed me. I was still reveling in my aloneness and my freedom. Although I met a few men who were also at that stage, I met *some* who were ready for marriage.

The first man I dated after my divorce was a highly successful businessman, who had been written up in the *Wall Street Journal* for his exploits. He was fun, interesting, and made no bones about the fact that he was shopping for a wife. He had been a widower for five years, was tired of the singles scene, and wanted to share his life with someone. I, on the other hand, had not even moved out of my marital home, didn't know where I was going or what it was like to be single and free, and was certainly not looking to tie myself to one person. So although we liked each other and saw a lot of each other for about three months, it didn't work out. He eventually met someone who was in the same stage as he, and they married.

The more I talked with other men and women, the more impressed I became with the importance of timing as a factor in how, when, and whom we marry. It is one of the most, if not *the* most important factor of all.

If you can catch my husband in a serious moment, perhaps he will tell you that the main reason he was still a bachelor at age fifty-two was not that he didn't *want* to marry. It was because when he was willing and ready, the other person wasn't, and when the other person was—you get the idea! *I* feel that when a man is ready to marry, it almost doesn't matter who is around at the time. If she's willing, she's the gal who will become his Mrs. On the other hand, two people may be ideally suited to one another, but if their lives are out of sync, nothing will help. Inevitably they'll drift apart.

If you and the man you're seeing turn out to be synchronized, you can proceed with your efforts to wed. Remember when I said that the needs of men and women are more alike than different? <u>Think about what makes a man lovable to you, and try to be those things to your man.</u> What I think is lovable in a man is affection, consideration, generosity, sexiness, cleanliness, intelligence, wit, and looking out for my interests, so I tried to be that way in return.

Can't you be more specific? I need step-by-step instructions!
Sure. Be nurturing. Take care of him. Show lots of concern for his comfort and well-being within the limits of your time. Make him comfortable in your home. Be interested in his problems and support his endeavors. Rub his back, massage his feet, pour cream into his coffee.

I can hear you now, screaming, "What about me? Who is going to take care of me? I work just as hard as he does, if not harder." Guess what? When you do these things for your guy, he reciprocates. You'll be surprised how your man will pamper you if you do it first.

But you mustn't keep score. It's not a tit-for-tat situation. You're simply giving and caring for its own sake. I was, and found that every man that I spent time with treated me with the utmost consideration in return. They took me out to dinner even when I offered to cook, *they* even cooked for *me*, they helped me buckle my shoes, they rubbed my back, helped me with my work if they could, bought me presents, took me on trips and shopping excursions—and one man even shaved my legs! I don't think my experience is unique or that I'm special or different from any of you.

One note of caution—your attitude will be obvious. If you're only doing these things to get your man instead of with genuine concern, it becomes manipulation, and he will know that you're a phony. We're talking here about a guy you genuinely care about and want to marry and take care of forever. There's a difference.

That's a tall order. What else?
The point is you shouldn't be just a taker. *Give* once in a while. If he has taken you out a lot, cook for him occasionally. Buy some good wine, and take the trouble to fix his favorite food. Buy him gifts within your means. If you see that he doesn't have a nice robe (or needs an extra one for your home), or needs a decent salad bowl, or talks about a record or book he would like to own, surprise him with it. Make a fuss about his birthday. Ask him what he would like to do, and arrange it, or please him with a dinner party for his friends and children. Help him in his business if you have connections that will throw some business his way. If he needs a job, help him find one. (But don't interfere in his business unless he invites you to. Men are very territorial about their jobs and resent women who tell them how to do it.) Remember that all this had to be done with subtlety, as some men dislike being fussed over by a woman.

Don't smother him. Don't question his whereabouts twenty-four hours a day. Don't call him constantly. Let him see that he will have autonomy and space after you're married, and that *you* aren't overly dependent. He may be concerned about his loss of freedom, so show him that he'll still be free to pursue his interests after marriage. (This excludes chasing women, however!) Don't intrude on his life. Give him the same respect you would any friend. Never go to his house without calling first—you wouldn't want him to do that to you, either. Don't call his friends to question them about him or his activities.

Remain autonomous until you're married. That means handling your own financial affairs. If he's spending a lot of time at your home and eating meals frequently with you, it's OK for you to expect him to contribute money to the household. It isn't fair for him to have no air conditioning, heating, or food costs when you do. (Unless you have no financial concerns.) If your cleaning woman does his laundry, be sure that he pays her extra for doing it. If you take his clothes to the cleaner, let him reimburse you. If you have children and he wants to take them places or buy them things, that's all right. But don't be a greedy, grasping woman, always dropping hints about what you need. If he is at all sensitive, he will see what you need help with, and will offer. Then you can decide whether or not you wish to accept.

Become indispensable in his life. Men are creatures of habit and love their comfort. Sooner or later he will become used to you and your loving ways. After he eats with you, talks to you, and sleeps with you, his bed and his home will seem awfully empty without you. Encourage him to tell you his troubles and talk over decisions. Find a way to give him the message that you will not be a burden to him, but want to share the responsibilities and problems that come with marriage. Many men stay in marriages long past the time when they love or even like their wives, because they like the routine and comfort of their lives and don't like change. This can work in *your* favor, as well. Become familiar, but not boring. The way to avoid being boring is to continue to live that interesting life you created for yourself as a single woman.

Wit and humor also come in here. Be spontaneous; use your ingenuity to do things that will keep him a little off balance. Above all, avoid looking desperate. Desperation is a major turn-off for men. Again, the best way to do this is to maintain a life of your own apart from him.

If premarital sex is acceptable to your beliefs, become the best lover you know how to be. Learn what pleases him, and be generous about giving pleasure to this number-one man in your life. Now is the time for you two to explore your sexuality together, and to discover all the erotic pleasures that are possible with a loving partner.

If he wants you to travel with him, I think you should only do so on nonbusiness trips. If he wants you to attend the national convention of his trade association, I suggest that you don't go. I went to one with Leonard and met many of his friends and business associates, but in casual conversations I heard them refer to some of the women at the meeting in this fashion: "Oh, she slept with So-and-so," or "Yeah, she's his girlfriend and has been traveling with him for years." Believe me, the tone of voice they used was *not* flattering. What bothered me most was that my husband, who was then just my "boyfriend," joined in these conversations with gusto. Then and there I decided I would not accompany him on any more business trips, but only on pleasure trips where we were not likely to encounter his colleagues.

Guess what happened? He stopped going to the meetings when I wouldn't go with him. He missed going, but he didn't want to leave me. I think this may have been a further incentive for him to think about marrying me. You may have some concern that if *you* don't go he'll take someone else. Let him—you will be more highly valued in the end. Let *her* be the subject of gossip!

If you both have children, make an attempt to bring the children together in trial situations. He will be reassured to know that it will work out all right. Work at establishing harmony between his and your kids. Let him know that you're aware of his financial responsibilities to his first family, and don't make snide remarks about their demands or his ex-wife's demands. Keep your feelings about her to yourself, even if you have to grit your teeth. He doesn't want to look ahead to friction between you two or between the families. Keep in mind that by being understanding and making him happy, you will be happy too.

Should we live together?
NO! (I can hear the screams and shouts of protest now.) My definition of living together is that one of you does not maintain his or her own home. If he sleeps with you every night but keeps most of his clothes and possessions in his own home, you are not living together by my definition.

The only reason to live together, in my opinion, is if you do *not* want to be married. Living together is one possible life style for a single person. But since we have established that *you* want to be married, living together is excluded as an option. Besides, it has not proved to be a valid test of whether a marriage will work. Many couples of the liberated sixties lived together for years, and when they finally married, the marriage did not work out. There is a subtle difference between the finality of marriage and the experience of living together. Many things depend on the commitment—inheritance rights, pension rights, and parental rights. To quote Jesse Bernard, "Without a commitment, one has freedom but not security; with a commitment, one has security but little freedom." If all you want is a lover, boyfriend, or steady, live together with my blessing, but this is a book about *remarriage*.

It does happen sometimes that a man or a woman is fearful about marriage, and living together can be a way to get comfortable with the idea. But in my view, it's still too risky. It takes you out of circulation. You have none of the status or rights of marriage, and none of the fun and freedom of dating. It can also be confusing for young children if someone lives with you and then leaves. As long as your man has a home that he returns to, they will be aware that he may not be in their lives forever, and subconsciously they will be prepared for his departure. It will still be hard for them, but not as hard as if the man were living with them on a day-to-day basis. If *you* move into *his* house, you lose your autonomy and are not free to leave when you want to.

You'll do as you like, of course, but after much study and contemplation this is the best advice I can give you. Many people disagree with me because they have had an unhappy marriage and feel that living together gives them a chance to determine whether a marriage with "this person" will work. Still, you can learn just as much about a person if you don't share the same roof, but spend many days and nights together, travel together, and so forth. I'm not saying what my grandma used to say: "If a man can get all the milk he wants, why should he buy the cow?" I'm saying, "If he never experiences what it's like to be without you, how can he appreciate how much you mean to him?"

What if I do all these things and he still doesn't mention marriage?
Let's hope that sooner or later he will decide he doesn't want to live without you, and bring up the subject. If he doesn't, you'll have to get some space between you so he can experience what it's like being without you.

I had a six-month timetable in mind when Leonard and I were dating. I already knew that I loved him, and since we were spending every day together, I felt it was fruitless to belabor the point if he couldn't decide that he loved me and wanted to marry me after 180 days and nights together. Occasionally I mentioned that I did not plan to have any more "one-year relationships" that went nowhere, and I feel that this was an important factor in his asking me to marry him. He certainly would not have been in a hurry otherwise; he was very comfortable and happy as things were, and, as a long-time bachelor, was used to living alone.

Several of the women I interviewed had to stop seeing the men they loved because the men just did not want to get married. It was difficult for them, and hurt a great deal. Eventually some of the men came to realize that these women were important to them, and did propose marriage. Other women I talked to were the reluctant ones, but their men gave *them* an ultimatum, either marriage or an end to the relationship.

If he still doesn't mention marriage, what do you do next? You can do several things. You can call him and arrange a meeting to discuss things with him. At this point there's nothing to lose. Let him know how you feel, and that you're interested in marrying him, if he doesn't know it already. If he indicates to you that *he* is not interested, it's time to move on. I do know women who have hung around for many years waiting for a man to decide to marry them. For some of them it worked; for others, it didn't. It is a risk, as you are out of circulation during that time.

These are your choices: get some space between you to see if he is motivated to ask you; discuss it with him to let him know that this is what you want; if his decision is negative, stay around, hoping he'll change his mind; or move on to look for someone new. I don't believe in manipulative games, lying, or entrapment schemes. They constitute a bad beginning for a marriage.

I want to reassure you once more that there's more than one man for you in this world. There are many potential partners out there. I found that since I did not meet men through my work, it usually took two months to meet someone else. For you it may be a shorter period of time. You *can* live without this man, and still continue to live the interesting life you have established for yourself while keeping your eye out for someone else. <u>You may feel depressed and lonely, but you will survive.</u> You may go through separation grief similar to what you experienced when you divorced or were widowed, and it will be almost as painful. <u>But you will have learned something</u>, and your life will be richer from this relationship. You'll have gained one more layer of depth and wisdom.

Thanks to the men I loved for a while, my life was opened up to new books, words, wines, foods, business, fishing, horse racing, dogs, travel, and sex. I never felt that the time I spent with these men was wasted. I also learned more about what I required to be happy, which helped me to know when I finally met the right man.

There *is* a new husband out there for you. Try not to compromise your standards because you're afraid of loneliness. You are a worthwhile, loving woman with a lot to give, and the next man down the road will appreciate it. And if you both agree to marry, you'll be off on a new adventure!

Here are some real-life examples of how women were asked to marry. I'll start off with my own:

Leonard and I had been seeing each other nearly every day for six months. We got along great, and I was in love with him. He would never admit that he loved me, although he always acted as though he did. Every year he went away on a business trip in the spring, and this year was no different. Off he went to New York. He called me every night while he was away, and did not enjoy the trip as much as he had in the past because he missed me.

When he came back, I had him over for dinner. He says it was the menu that got him—hamburgers with onions and sautéed mushrooms, home-fried potatoes, a great salad, and good wine. After dinner he looked at me and admitted that he loved me.

A few weeks later, after picking me up at the dentist's office, we went to Howard Johnson's for coffee. Across the table at Ho-Jo's he said, "Well, I guess the next step is we should get married." And that's just what we did three years ago!

Here are a few other real-life experiences:

"Fred and I had gone out for three years. He was a long-time bachelor and didn't want to get married. I had two little boys, and every summer when they went away to camp, he would break up with me. I guess he was afraid of too much closeness. After our third breakup, I had a big barbecue for Labor Day and invited all his relatives. He couldn't stand being left out, and showed up. He asked me if I wanted to get together again, and I said no. I was tired of his ambivalence and couldn't take it anymore. So he said, 'OK. Do you want to get engaged? We're engaged.' And that's how *I* got proposed to!"

"Les and I went together for two years and were very much in love. During this time, though, he was getting his divorce, and when he was finally free, he felt that he was trapped and had never experienced single life. I said 'bye-bye' and we both dated other people.

"After a few months, he called me and said that he was wrong and he wanted to get married. We still had a few problems to work out, but I guess he realized how hard it was to find someone out there in the world who cared about him as much as I did—he had to see for himself. I think most men and women just don't realize how long it takes to form a good, close relationship. Time spent with one another, and the things you share form a bond that's hard to duplicate when you just run around 'having fun.' We're happily married now, and enjoying it more than either of us thought we would."

"I met Gary on a trip. He was working out of the country and I was in the travel business. We had instant chemistry, and he flew back to the United States to visit me as often as he could. He had been married twice before, and was leery about marriage. My family was leery about *him* because of his previous marriages, but we were in love, and after we had been seeing each other for about a year, I told him that I wanted us either to get married or to stop seeing each other. He asked me to be a little more patient, as he had to work out some things with his ex-wives and his children. He did, and we married soon after. I'm so much happier in this marriage. We do everything together, and have a closeness that I never had with my first husband."

"I had been widowed a short time when friends introduced me to Ken. I wasn't lonely at all, and didn't want to get married again. After three years of seeing each other, though, he gave me an ultimatum one day. He wanted to get married, and if I didn't, he wasn't going to see me anymore. I couldn't stand the thought of being without him, so here I am, much to my surprise, a married woman again."

"After I was divorced, I really didn't try to get married again. I met Louis at a party given by mutual friends, and he just became a part of my life. I have two small children and he has one, and I must admit that I did worry about combining the two families. He spent most evenings at my house, and once a week we would go out. It just seemed natural for us to get married, because we fell in love. We went together for about two years, and he was the only man I dated."

Here's a little summary for you of my thoughts on how to find the right man for you and then, after you've found him, how to end up marrying him.

1. Be honest with yourself about the kind of man and life style that you want.

2. Read your men. Don't deceive yourself into thinking that they're something other than they really are.

3. Remember, no one changes his basic character permanently—only long enough to woo and wed you.

4. Every man has a tragic flaw, so choose a man whose flaws you can tolerate.

5. Beware of the types of "wrong men" I have described for you.

6. It is not only acceptable but very common for people to marry for reasons other than mad, passionate love. Mutual caring and commitment are an excellent basis for marriage.

7. Remember, men *like* to be married.

8. Timing is all-important in whether you marry a specific man. Be sure that your lives are synchronized before you set your sights on marriage.

9. Be nurturing, giving, and loving and he will be, too.

10. Don't smother him.

11. Remain autonomous until marriage and do not live together.

12. Become indispensable in his life.

13. Become the best lover you can.

14. Reassure him in subtle ways that you want to share the responsibilities of marriage with him and will not be a burden.

15. Try to establish harmony between your families once your relationship has become serious.

16. If he doesn't seem interested in marriage after a significant period of time—get some space between you.

17. If he never changes his mind, let go and move on. There's more than one man in this world for you.

18. Don't get discouraged. *There is a husband for you out there!*

Let's move on now, and take a look at the exciting but stressful realm of remarriage.

CHAPTER SEVEN

The Wedding and Beyond: A New Life Together

As you get closer and closer to remarriage, all kinds of questions, fears, and concerns will arise, along with the excitement and happiness of joining the world of the married once more. It's normal to get cold feet. After the time and effort you've invested in readjusting to single life, you may awaken one day to find that you are loath to give up your new life style. You may be enjoying new feelings of independence and strength, and the idea of having to share your life again may give you pause. Besides, there are all those other relationships that must be managed in order to blend your two families into one.

If you do have ambivalent feelings, remember that they're perfectly normal. Jesse Bernard feels that we want opposite things in life: variety *and* security, stability *and* adventure, excitement *and* a quiet haven to retreat to. When you wonder whether you can handle the challenges of a new marriage, you're just being human. Making a life together requires planning, preparation, discussion, great patience, and a strong desire on your part and your man's but it's worth it!

Most people love their remarriage. They're thrilled to

be establishing a new life with a partner, and they agree
that the results justify the efforts. But a new marriage does
require flexibility and a willingness to work together to
overcome any obstacles.

Why do people remarry?

By and large, people are more comfortable living a traditional life style. Marriage is a public avowal of their relationship, and the world takes it more seriously than when
two people are just lovers or living together. It provides
more emotional security—both partners can dart out from
the safety of the marriage to try new things with more confidence than if they were alone. This is a natural feeling,
which goes back to the security we felt as children with our
mothers. And if there are children, the parent wishes to
provide them with some stability, which is harder when
love relationships come and go. There's also the desire to
have a partner in life, even if you know you're capable of
going it alone.

Here are some of the reasons given to me by women
who have remarried:

"I wanted companionship and financial security."

"I fell in love with my present husband."

"My friends were getting married, I thought the money
situation would be much better, and I wanted companionship and love."

"I was lonely, afraid of the future alone, and believed
that I had found someone to share my life with."

"I was in love and felt that we had the potential for a
good life together."

Why is it that some people never remarry, then?

There can be many reasons. They may prefer the single life,

and know that they want to be accountable only to themselves. The thought of sharing their lives again may make them anxious; perhaps they have an aversion to sex, have been disappointed in love, or are less worried about being alone than about risking an intimate relationship with another person.

Hasn't marriage also had a bad press?

Although people have always sought out a married life style, many negative comments about marriage *have* found their way into the literature of the ages. What do I mean? Here are some examples from the pages of time.

> Socrates: " 'By all means, marry. If you will get for yourself a good wife, you will be happy forever after, and if by chance you get a common scold like my Xanthippe—why then you will become a philosopher.' When asked which was preferable, to take or not to take a wife, he replied, 'Whichever a man does, he will repent it.' "

> La Rochefoucauld: "There are good marriages, but there are no delightful ones."

> Ambrose Bierce: "Marriage is a community consisting of a master, a mistress, and two slaves, making in all, two."

> Francis Bacon (when asked about the most suitable age at which a man should marry): "The young man not yet, the old man not at all."

> George Bernard Shaw: "When two people are under the influence of the most violent, most insane, most delusive, and most transient of passions, they are required to swear that they will remain in that excited, abnormal, and exhausting condition continuously until death do us part."

To offset this negative propaganda are several thoughts in favor of marriage.

Goethe: "A wife is a gift bestowed upon a man to reconcile him to the loss of Paradise."

Henry Ward Beecher: "When men enter into the state of marriage, they stand nearest to God."

John Lyly: "Marriages are made in heaven and consumma-ted on earth."

Despite the mixed press, 2,495,000 marriages took place in the United States in 1982, 2% more than in 1981, showing an increase for the seventh consecutive year. Also, four out of five divorces in the United States still end in remarriage. Although American remarriages are no more successful than first marriages in their divorce rate, this appears to be because people are less reluctant to divorce after they have done it once. One thing most remarried folk do agree on: whether or not the marriage lasts, the *quality* of their remar-riage is better.

sweet lemon ?

Besides, as I said in Chapter One, marriage is definite-ly a *healthier* way of life for you. An article in the *New York Times* (May 8, 1979) stated that according to statistics, being married and living with one's spouse, regardless of the quality of the relationship, is the healthiest of marital states, although the actual act of marrying is a stressful life event that often causes temporary illness. (In fact, four out of five newlyweds get sick.) There are definite health haz-ards to being single, according to the *Times*, such as smok-ing more, drinking more, more illness, more cancer of the digestive system, and a higher number of admissions to psychiatric hospitals. And according to an article in the *American Sociological Review*, the "advantages of marriage are especially apparent when life circumstances are the most difficult, not when they are most benign. Marriage can function as a protective barrier against the distressful consequences of outside threats. It doesn't prevent economic and social problems from invading life, but can help fend off the psychological assaults such problems otherwise create. Even in an era when it is often a 'fragile arrangement' its capacity to protect people from the full impact of external strains makes it surprisingly stable."

In all fairness, though, I must tell you that many writers share the opinion that marriage is healthier for men than for women, including Jesse Bernard, who has made an intensive study of marriage. Perhaps this is because wives often have to make more adjustments in marriage. More women than men consider their marriage unhappy, and twice as many wives as husbands state that they would not remarry the same partner. More married women than single have nervous breakdowns, phobias, depressions, and psychiatric disturbances, and they also commit more crimes. More wives than husbands initiate divorces and counseling, but this may be because women are more willing to seek help when they need it. The age-old stereotypes of the frustrated old maid and the happy bachelor are completely false. The truth is just the opposite.

Our previously mentioned anonymous Canadian woman wrote facetiously: "The most noteworthy thing to be said about marriage is that it improves men. Even the most mediocre specimen will, with the addition of a wife, suddenly blossom into a smiling, silver-sideburned sophisticate. He begins each day well-rested, well-fed, well-dressed, and well and truly pleased with himself. His ambition vaults, his earning capacity trebles, and he is now the Provider, centered and purposeful. In short, marriage *makes* men."

She goes on to explain, however, how women's lives take a plunge. The dissolution starts with the husband "coming up with Ways to Improve Yourself (the points he wishes to improve are the same ones he found so attractive in the first place), then goes downhill with you becoming

immersed in *his* life and how to improve it, and the mother-
hood phase with all its unglamorous aspects, and then . . .
deadly boredom only alleviated by lunches with the girls,
work, exercise classes and love affairs."

This is obviously obsolete thinking, as today's woman
is rarely immersed in her husband's life; she has interests
and a life of her own. But it's one more example of the per-
sisting perceptions of women's and men's roles in a marriage. Many a busy, overworked, married career woman of
today wails half-jokingly, "What I need is a housewife!"

What will another marriage really be like?

It will be different from the first. There may be problems,
but no matter how difficult they are, most people agree that
they are far outweighed by the benefits. For example,
someone once referred to remarriage as involving a "cast of
thousands," which means that you will have emotional
and legal ties to a lot of people. There may be intrusions,
demands, and complaints from former spouses, children,
and ex-in-laws. The solution is to make sure that you and
your man discuss these problems beforehand, and have a
basis for communication about them. You will be encouraged to note that most people passionately enjoy their
remarriage. For one thing, both partners are more experienced and usually know what they want. For another, you
are both presumably grown up and "finished," and you
can see what you're getting. You are what you are, whether
it is bald, fat, poor, or rich. He knows if you like wines or
jazz, are an outdoor or indoor person, and you know a lot
about him.

Women are more comfortable being themselves in a remarriage, and can really appreciate having someone to care
about them after fending for themselves for a while. They
have struggled to make a life alone, and are more aware of
how it feels to work and come home tired, while men have

had a chance to get familiar with the kitchen. Also, sex is usually better. Both partners are less uptight, have no doubt learned something about orgasm, and have less fear of pregnancy because they are more familiar with birth-control methods (he may have had a vasectomy). They have usually tested their sexual compatibility before marriage, and are likely to be more experimental and less inhibited than they were in their first marriage.

Also, we remarrieds are more open about our feelings and don't tend to keep things inside as much. (Part of this stems from not being afraid to lose our spouse through another divorce.) We are also more realistic, and don't expect perfection and romance all the time, and we're more tolerant. For the sake of the relationship we don't mind doing things we may not enjoy ourselves, if it means a lot to our partner. (For instance, I go around the golf course with my husband because I know he enjoys having me there, even though it isn't my favorite activity.) Remarrieds are grateful that they have found a companion and a partner, and they try harder. We also tend to keep our sense of humor alive, a valuable asset in a marriage. Most remarrieds are passionately in love with each other, and their renewed sex life and vitality are a real bonus.

My second marriage is almost totally unlike my first. Not only is my husband the polar opposite of my first husband, but our life together is different. One of the biggest differences is that we are free of child-rearing responsibilities, as my children are grown and living independently, and Leonard has no children. Occasionally, crises arise in the children's lives and we may become involved, but the day-to-day responsibilities are just not there. We are also both in our middle years, when we appreciate the finiteness of things and are determined to appreciate our health and our life while we can. Even my husband's new business venture, a travel agency, was chosen because it provides enjoyment along with a business challenge.

I am still surprised at times when Leonard reacts to things differently from my previous husband, even though we have been married for a while now. I have to remind myself occasionally that he is a different person, and that I can count on that difference. In this marriage I'm also more open about my feelings. I no longer withdraw or sulk when I'm angry—I learned the hard way that it only hurts me and my relationships when I hold things back. At the same time, I don't react to things so strongly anymore, as I am less concerned with minor matters. This is all part of being older and more mature, I'm sure, but life is now certainly more serene and just plain good.

But what about those of us who have children still dependent on us? How will they affect my marriage?
Remarriages with children living at home are quite different from remarriages without. If both of you have children who are living with you, your big task will be to blend both families into a whole. This will take time and great patience on your part, as well as cooperation from your spouse and the absentee parents. Resentments may be a typical part of the scenario; you can count on the children to watch like hawks for signs of favoritism. Sometimes, in order not to favor your own children, you may bend too far the other way and be nicer to the stepchildren. Needless to say, your own kids will resent this, and they will hit you with accusations at every opportunity. It's sort of a "lose-lose" proposition with the stepchildren too, because if you're nice they think you're trying to replace their "real" mother, and if you're not, you're the wicked stepmother. His children may also have had a different upbringing regarding the expression of emotions, and your reactions may seem strange to them. You may be a hugger and a kisser, for instance, but their previous experience doesn't include this.

Then there's the matter of discipline. Most stepparents

find that it takes time to feel comfortable disciplining a child who is not theirs, but eventually they must come to an agreement on a consistent policy and stand united in the way that all the children in the family are disciplined.

Even if the children live with their mother and just visit, they may try not to like you so as not to be disloyal to their own mother. You must make an effort to see their point of view. The children in a new marriage are asked to make many adjustments; not only do they have to adjust to a new stepparent, but often to living in a new home and with new siblings. In most cases *your* children have gotten to know your new husband well during the courtship, but his children may not have had the same opportunity to know *you*. Even if you only see his children on weekends, they can cause a lot of disruption with telephone calls during the rest of the week and with the mayhem they may create when they visit. Also, in many cases, his children start out living with their mother, but decide after a while that they want to live with you. Often, once the biological mother experiences the everyday responsibilities of rearing a child alone, she may be only too eager to dump the child or children on you, especially if she perceives that they are interfering with her chances at remarriage or romance. You must be prepared for this eventuality when you marry a man with minor children.

It is extremely important that you maintain good communication with both previous spouses in matters concerning the children. You may detest each other, but these feelings must be set aside in the interests of peace. Children can be manipulative and ask both sets of parents for the same thing, or when they come to visit they may lie about what they are allowed to do at home, and the other way around. Kids love to test you, but you will be on firm ground if all sets of parents have agreed on how the children will be handled.

Some stepchildren do not want or need a close relationship with you, and you must accept this too, rather than trying to change their minds. If closeness is going to develop, it will happen without your forcing it.

What about the issue of what to call stepparents or how to introduce them? "Step" has such a negative connotation that it really needs to be replaced by a better term. It's also unrealistic to expect the children to call you "Mom" or your new husband "Dad," as the case may be, even if the real parent is deceased. The child will eventually come up with a term that is acceptable to him or her. Most families tend to use the first name of the stepparent as a good compromise. Of course, the last name is not changed unless the child is legally adopted by the stepfather.

Some couples will decide to have another child together, which sometimes helps to synthesize the family. It depends on the previous number of children. Families can grow very large and cumbersome, especially if each partner has had several marriages. Many couples do not wish to add to their already numerous responsibilities.

The children's ages influence the ease with which they assimilate into the new living situation. Younger children adjust more easily and are more accepting of a new parent, while adolescents can be quite rebellious. In interviews, adolescents will admit that at first they were obnoxious to their stepparent, but now love, appreciate, and respect them and are grateful that the family did not give up on them.

Children may be disruptive, but they are part of the deal, and most couples want the marriage enough to put up with the disruption. Eventually they manage to have a good family life that includes the kids. Money can aggravate the situation; a new wife may feel angry or deprived when she has to lower her standard of living to provide for her husband's first family. In addition, she may be deeply upset if she is contributing to the support of the household and sees the money going to a wife who doesn't work. Again, great maturity, commitment, and love are necessary to keep a new marriage from going sour over these kinds of things.

Sometimes a stepfather assumes total financial responsibility for his stepchildren when the real father does not meet *his* responsibilities. Lucile Duberman of Rutgers University surveyed 100 men with stepchildren under the age of twenty-one and found that 69% of them paid all the expenses, 19% paid part, and only 12% paid none. That is, 69% of the "real" fathers paid no support for their children. If a woman has money, she will often pay for her children's expenses, but if she doesn't, who pays for what can be touchy. Make an effort to discuss these issues beforehand and come to an understanding of how to face them. You'll save yourselves a lot of strife and bitterness. Most spouses find reasonable solutions to all these problems, so don't be discouraged. Consider them challenges to your love and your intelligence.

What about former spouses? Are they usually problems?
Former spouses can be lethal to your new marriage if you allow them to be. You may feel jealous if your husband has to interact a great deal with his former wife, just as he may feel jealous of your former husband. Ex's may complain and make demands, or even actively intrude on your lives. Sometimes *they* are jealous of your relationship with their children. For fear that you will replace them in their children's affections, they will try to undermine you. You will also have to keep a sense of humor when your husband calls you by his former wife's name—it will happen at least once! Even if she is dead, you are not immune to jealousy. You may be reminded constantly that the former couple always did things in a certain established way, but with time, the new life style will take precedence. Be patient.

It's ideal for everyone concerned if ex's can be friends, but this is rare. Everyone should at least try to be civil, however, since sometimes you will have to be together at family events such as graduations, funerals, and weddings, and it's better if you all get along. My former husband barely speaks to me, but under duress he will say hello if I initiate it. In the year following our divorce, two of our daughters got married and we went through the two weddings, even marching down the aisle together, but he wouldn't speak to me. I, however, was (and am) determined not to let his attitude interfere with any happy occasions, so we generally ignore each other when we have to be present at the same event. My advice is to try to establish some sort of neutrality that will allow people to feel comfortable when they invite you both to the same parties. If coolness persists, however, as in my situation, accept the reality and don't let it interfere with your attendance at festive gatherings.

Where is it best to live, in his house or mine?
The decision about where to live may not be easy, but it need not be a major crisis. Let me tell you our story.

I owned a one-bedroom condominium apartment and my husband owned a townhouse in a suburb of the city. He also had a bulldog that he loved, who was eleven years old at the time (she was ferocious-looking and fat, but her name was "Puppy"). We liked my building and decided to buy a larger apartment in it together. I was able to sell my apartment rather quickly, but then we found out that the dog was not allowed to live in the building. It seemed that existing dog residents were "grandfathered" in, but no new animals were being accepted as tenants.

We decided to live in the townhouse and put the *new* apartment up for sale. Just at that time, the housing market in Miami fell into a slump and we were unable to sell at our price, so we found ourselves paying two mortgages: a financial nightmare. Then we decided to put both homes on the market, see which sold first, and let fate decree where we would live. As fate would have it, my husband's townhouse sold first at a decent price, so then we were faced with the problem of what to do with the dog. After much agonizing, we found a home for her with a family of confirmed bulldog lovers, where we tearfully left her to spend her last days in luxury.

During this time we went through two major moves and two remodelings. First, when I sold my condo and moved to the townhouse, we worked like beavers to fix it up. Then, nine months later, we had to make another major move (twelve years' accumulation of Leonard's stuff) into the apartment, where we also did a major remodeling job. Two nights before the wedding we were so exhausted we could hardly move. We were still moving clothes and things from my place to his at 11:00 p.m. The moral is never to underestimate the residence decision, and try to plan ahead to avoid last-minute craziness. You don't want to be a tired, cranky bride.

Keep in mind that if either of you moves into the other's home, you will be living with the accumulated memories that the house represents. This is usually more bothersome to women than to men, since the woman is traditionally the keeper of the home. If she lives in another woman's former household, she faces everyday reminders that "she" did it differently, and unless the home is redecorated, she lives with "her" things. One of my friends (she refers to herself as a "geriatric bride," since she wed for the first time at age sixty-eight) married a widower and moved into his home. About four years after their marriage, she managed to redecorate. When I asked her what advice she could give us, she said, "Have a giant garage sale." She was only half kidding.

You could wait a while, though, as you don't want to

hit a new spouse over the head with too many changes at once. Gradually, over time, you will be able to make the home "yours." I know women and men who have moved into their previously married spouses' homes and are quite comfortable and happy, but if you're uncomfortable, it doesn't pay to have this negative influence on your marriage. The aforementioned second wife also inherited the first wife's maid, who refers to her former mistress as "the real Mrs. Smith." (Fortunately my friend has a terrific sense of humor!)

If there are children involved, you will also have to take their needs into consideration. It's always advisable to make as few drastic changes as possible in their lives, so try not to make them change schools and leave friends unless it is absolutely necessary. Some divorce agreements may also have restrictions about how far you can take children from their other parent's home.

Finances and proximity to your workplace will dictate where you live, to a great extent. In today's world of high mortgage rates and rents, it would be nice to hang on to a house with a low mortgage or a rent-controlled apartment, if possible, especially if it's in a convenient location for all of you. In our case location wasn't important, as Leonard had sold his business just before we married.

Another facet of the complex living situation is who owns the property. New wives, no doubt, would rather have their home in both names instead of just one, but it's unrealistic to expect a new spouse to do this right away, especially when there are children who are heirs to the property. Buying a new home that can be in both your names is an attractive alternative. In that case, however, both spouses are usually expected to contribute to the cost. Often, after a few years of marriage, when trust has had a chance to build, the spouse who owns the property will put it in both names out of a desire to protect the other spouse when he or she dies. This is a loving gesture, but is not mandated by law in most states.

This seems to be an appropriate place to discuss prenuptial contracts. They are becoming more and more popular, as they often prevent misunderstandings and resentment. I know one instance, though, where the contract almost prevented the wedding from taking place. The bride-to-be was infuriated when she saw the contract that the groom's attorney had drawn up, and called off the wedding. The couple was married eventually, but a lot of angry feelings had been generated, which cast a pall over what should have been a very happy time.

In other instances I know of, the agreement eased the minds of both the bride and the groom, who were concerned about protecting their children's rights or alleviating their grown children's fears about whether their parent's fortune would go to the new spouse. You and your future husband should consider such matters and make your decision. Each person should have his own attorney either look the contract over or help to draw it up. Always include a provision for new goods that are accumulated by the couple after their marriage.

Is planning a second wedding more difficult than the first?
I don't think so—in fact, I think it's even more fun! You two can do exactly what you want instead of pleasing your parents, as you may have had to do the first time around.

It is, however, a more complex undertaking. For example, this letter recently ran in an Ann Landers' column.

Dear Ann:
A few weeks ago I clipped a cartoon by Signe Wilkinson of the San Jose *Mercury News* that put me in stitches. That cartoon depicted the modern wedding party. Each person

had a number and the identification appeared in a 'key' be-
low. It's difficult to explain in words what a cartoon looks
like, but I'll do my best.

The drawing showed (1) Bride, (2) Groom, (3) Groom's
daughter from first marriage, (4) Bride's mother, (5) Bride's
mother's current lover, (6) Bride's sperm donor father, (7
and 8) Sperm donor's parents who sued for visitation rights,
(9) Bride's mother's lover at time of bride's birth, (10)
Groom's mother, (11) Groom's mother's boyfriend, (12)
Groom's father, (13) Groom's stepmother, (14) Groom's father's third wife, (15) Groom's grandfather, (16) Groom's
grandfather's lover, (17) Groom's first wife.

The letter is signed Planet Earth, 1983. As far fetched as this
letter sounds, I can think of a few more people who could
have been in the picture, such as additional children, previous spouses, and grandchildren.

Humor aside, these are some of the things you really *do*
have to take into consideration for your wedding in addition to the guest list:

The date

What kind of ceremony you want

Where it will be

What kind of reception you want, where it should be
held, and who is going to pay for it

Do you want attendants?

How are you going to dress?

How are you going to word the invitations?

What role will the children play?

Are you going to take a wedding trip?

But before you decide *how* you are going to marry, you will have to break the news to your families. Since you two have no doubt been very close for some time now, the children and your friends and family are probably aware of your interest in each other, and will not be too surprised when you actually disclose the decision.

How should you do it? Some women prefer to sit down with their children, parents, or other close family members, together with their intended husband, to announce and discuss their wedding plans. Others prefer to do it alone. Remember that it's perfectly normal for your children to feel some ambivalence about your decision. While they may be happy for you, they also may have harbored fantasies about your reuniting with their father, and now these hopes are completely shattered. They may also be concerned about what will happen to them now that you are establishing a new life. Be prepared for all kinds of reactions and try to talk out everyone's feelings and bring them into the open. Sometimes initial reactions will change as the idea has time to sink in, so don't be discouraged if the children are not totally thrilled. You know what will be good for yourself and your children, and shouldn't let their understandable fears interfere with your happiness.

I chose to tell my children without Leonard present. They were all adults, and we had shared a lot of ups and downs over the years. I also wanted to give everyone an opportunity to speak freely with no constraints. So one Friday evening after work, I summoned my daughters—Leslie, Aimee, Wendy, and Cathy—and my son-in-law, Lance, to my apartment. I had a bottle of champagne on ice ready to pop open after the announcement. Leonard waited downstairs in the lobby of my building.

When I sat down in the living room with the kids, one of them announced casually, "We know we're here so you can tell us that you and Leonard are getting married." Well, that took the wind out of my sails, and all that was left to do was to discuss it a bit. Everyone was very happy, and we called downstairs for Leonard to come on up—the coast was clear. Meanwhile, Lance went down to his car, where he and Wendy had a bottle of champagne stashed with a card saying, "Congratulations, we are happy for you and love you." You can see how much I surprised *my* kids. Afterward we all went on to a gala evening of toasting, dancing, and fun.

On the other hand, Leonard decided to invite his family out to dinner and make the announcement with me there. So, off we went, his sister, mother, brother-in-law, and uncle. All through dinner I kept waiting, but no announcement. Every time I looked at Leonard, his eyes said, "Not now, not now." As each course came and went, we both grew more and more nervous.

Finally dinner was over and we all left the restaurant. We were saying good night in the parking lot when Leonard blurted out, "Rusty and I are getting married." Everyone was relieved, as they had been expecting it, and kisses and congratulations were exchanged all around. Again, no one was too surprised.

After you break the news, you will have to set a date. This sounds easier than it is. Something always gets in your way, such as holidays, the travel plans of important people you want to be present, the availability of sites for receptions, the schedule of the person you want to perform the ceremony, time off from jobs, children's schedules, or moving to a new home. When you finally do set the date, remember that it will take at least two weeks for your invitations to be printed and another week to gather all the addresses and mail them out. It still takes time even if you hand write your invitations or only phone the guests, so count on a longer period of time than you think necessary to plan your wedding.

Then you and your groom will have to decide on your mode of dress. Shopping for your dress is a nerve-wracking business, and you may have to look long and hard before you settle on your "look" and then find a dress that fits both your fantasy and your budget. The one hard-and-fast rule for second brides is to avoid a veil or any kind of apparel that seems to suggest that you have not been married before, although you can be as dressy as you like.

Along with all these other decisions, you'll have to decide what kind of wedding you want. Although kinds of wedding arrangements vary tremendously, most experts agree that second (or third, or whatever) weddings should be more informal than the first. You may want to have a wedding that's completely different from the first one; if your first wedding, for instance, was a hurried civil ceremony before your husband left for military service, you might want a large, gala affair this time. On the other hand, if you had all the frills the first time, you might opt for a more sedate affair. Many older brides seem to prefer a small private ceremony and then a larger reception, either the same day or at another time. You're not locked into any format, though. Express yourselves—do what you two really want to do. Part of the fun of marrying when you are older is that you're more comfortable with yourselves and in doing the things that make you happy. If you just want to run off and "elope," go ahead. If you want to be married on the high seas, while skydiving, or on a beach, by all means *do* it!

Now you have to decide how you will integrate the children into the occasion. Sometimes grown children serve as attendants or witnesses, and at other times they just stand around the couple during the ceremony. Anything you feel is right, will be right. The only definite "no-no" I found in my research was inviting former spouses to your wedding; otherwise just about anything goes.

Where to have it? There are many, many options. At home, at a hotel, in a church or synagogue, at a restaurant or catering hall, at a friend's home, and so on. Do try to make it as easy on yourselves as possible; you don't want to be all worn out on your wedding day and more nervous than you have to be. Cost is all-important, too. You will find it expensive to hold weddings outside your home, and catering is also very costly.

You and your groom will have to discuss how you are going to pay for the wedding, and who will bear the cost. Very often the groom will pay for the party, but if he is unable and the bride has means, she can assume the financial responsibility. Of course, you can also share the expenses. It's an entirely individual matter, as there are no hard-and-fast rules for a remarriage.

Here are a few examples of how some couples handled their wedding arrangements, starting with my own.

We discussed in detail what kind of wedding we wanted. It was very difficult to decide whether to just have the family and a few intimate friends or to have all our friends and family. It was either twenty people or seventy-five. We opted to invite all our friends and family to the reception because it was Leonard's first wedding, and to have just the family at the ceremony.

We considered all the possible places for the ceremony and the reception, and got dizzy from the possibilities. Finally we decided that we wanted to have the ceremony in a religious setting and to have the reception somewhere else, rather than have the ceremony at a restaurant or hotel. We're both pretty traditional people, and are both softies. With great difficulty and lots of telephoning and footwork, we were finally able to plan an August wedding in a rabbi's study (almost all the rabbis were going to be away on vacation that month) and a brunch reception at a private club.

We sent out printed invitations to the reception in our names, as we were the hosts of the affair, and included a separate card for those invited to the ceremony.

Leonard's uncle was his best man, and my sister was my attendant. My children and Leonard's family just stood around us (and cried). I wore a beige chiffon street-length dress with a crocheted jacket, and Leonard wore a medium gray business suit. At about 10:00 a.m. on a Sunday we all gathered at the study, where the ceremony was performed, and then we drove to the club, where we received the other guests at about 11:30. We had sixty-five guests in a private dining room, and everyone helped themselves to the lavish brunch set up for the club's usual Sunday morning buffet. Champagne was served to everyone, and the waiters took orders for other drinks during the party. We had a band, and a photographer was on hand to record this momentous event for posterity. It was a very sweet and solemn ceremony and a very happy party with lots of dancing, revelry, toasts, and general craziness, which is exactly what we wanted.

We had our suitcases in the car, and left directly from the party for a weekend in Palm Beach at our favorite hotel. A month later we took a longer trip to Europe.

My friend Marilyn, on the other hand, chose to have her second wedding at her home at 4:00 p.m. She invited everyone she and her fiancé knew, about a hundred people. Marilyn wore a long dress with no hat, and Norman, the groom, wore a suit and tie. Champagne was served before the ceremony while the guests gathered, and a clergyman married the couple in a religious ceremony. Marilyn's children were present, but just stood with the couple during the rites and had no formal part. Afterwards a catered buffet was served for dinner, and a bar and a band provided everyone with a great party. Their honeymoon weekend almost had to be canceled when the baby sitter pooped out, but at the last minute a relative volunteered for service, and off they went.

Another friend was married by a clergyman in her living room, with only their children and six close friends present. She wore a short dress and the groom wore a dark suit. After the ceremony champagne was served, and then everyone went out to dinner at a fine restaurant as guests of the couple.

Carlie and George were married by a clergyman at a hotel, with all their children and about fifty guests present. She wore a chiffon dress and picture hat, and the groom wore a light suit. They served a buffet lunch afterwards with champagne. There was no music, but the day was very festive. The couple then went to a local hotel for a few days.

My daughter, Leslie, remarried recently in a religious ceremony at her husband Marwin's home. The ceremony took place outdoors in the garden on a lovely sunny day, with both immediate families and a few intimate friends present. She wore an ankle-length batiste dress and no hat, and Marwin wore a dark suit. My daughter Wendy and I made hors d' oeuvres, which were served after the ceremony while the men in the family poured champagne. Since it was Thanksgiving Day, we all went out for Thanksgiving dinner in a private dining room at a lovely local restaurant. The couple then went off for a few days' honeymoon at a local hotel. A month later, on Christmas Eve, they held a large reception for about 250 people at their home, complete with music, a buffet dinner, and drinks—a beautiful, exciting, festive affair. Having the reception at a later date gave them a chance to plan it in a more relaxed manner.

So as you can see from these few examples, you can have just about any kind of wedding you wish. If you have your good friends and family around you, I guarantee that it will be a warm, loving, happy occasion. After the emotional and practical changes of your single years, you will be so thankful and joyous at the thought of starting a new phase of your life that you will be floating on air. You may find that this wedding is even more romantic and festive than your first. There are so many more facets to both your lives now, and you have friends and family that you didn't have the first time around.

You are certainly starting this marriage better prepared than you were the first time. You're more of a whole person, and you also have a sincere and overwhelming desire to make this one work better. The two of you have an understanding of each other that cannot be equaled by naive young things just embarking on life's adventures, but this does not diminish your love, caring, passion, and excitement one bit.

Many beautiful words have been written to express the bonds, loyalties, and love that a marriage can bring, but I was especially moved by these, which were spoken by Gerhard Neubeck at an annual meeting of the National Council on Family Relations:

> Here we are, helpmeets, spouses, mates, lovers, wives, husbands. We come in handy, don't we? We complement each other, we fit, we mesh, we mix, we dovetail, we trade and barter and exchange, we are one flesh. I do not want to knock other options but hurrah for marriage. Hurrah for building a history together. Hurrah for an institution that gives us that opportunity.

And, hurrah for you! You, too, will make it as a single and emerge with a new husband. Good luck, and be happy!

Bibliography

Abeel, Erica: *I'll Call You Tomorrow and Other Lies Between Men and Women*, William Morrow and Co., Inc., New York, 1981.

Barkas, J.L.: *Single in America*, Atheneum, New York, 1980.

Bernard, Jesse: *The Future of Marriage*, Yale University Press, New Haven, 1982

Bernard, Jesse: *Remarriage, A Study of Marriage*, The Dryden Press, New York, 1956.

Brody, Jane: "Marriage is Good for Health and Longevity, Studies Say," *New York Times*, May 8, 1979, p. C1.

Brody, Jane: *Jane Brody's Nutrition Book*, W.W. Norton and Co., New York, London, 1981.

Brothers, Joyce: *What Every Woman Should Know About Men*, Simon and Schuster, New York, 1981.

Casler, Laurence: *Is Marriage Necessary?*, Popular Library, New York, 1976.

Clinebell, Howard: *Understanding and Counseling the Alcoholic*, Abingdon Press, Nashville, 1968.

187

Comfort, Alex: *The Joy of Sex*, Simon and Schuster, New York, 1972.

Duberman, Lucile: *The Reconstituted Family*, Nelson Hall, Chicago, 1975.

Goldberg, Herb: *The Hazards of Being Male*, Nash Publishing, New York, 1976.

Hite, Shere: *The Hite Report: A Nationwide Study of Female Sexuality*, Dell, New York, 1976.

Hite, Shere: *The Hite Report on Male Sexuality*, Knopf, New York, 1981.

Holland, Hilda: *Why Are You Single?*, Farrar Straus and Co., New York, 1949.

Jenner, Heather and Segal, Muriel: *Men and Marriage*, G.P. Putnam's Sons, New York, 1970.

Joseph, Raymond A.: "American Men Find Asian Brides Fill the Unliberated Bill," *Wall Street Journal*, January 25, 1984, pp. 1 and 22.

Ledbetter, Les: "Jilted California Accountant Sues His Date for $38 in Expenses," *New York Times*, July 26, 1978, p. A10.

Mason, Robert Lee: *How to Choose the Wrong Marriage Partner and Live Unhappily Ever After*, John Knox Press, Atlanta, 1979.

Masters, William, and Johnson, Virginia: *Human Sexual Response*, Little, Brown, Boston, 1966.

Masters, William, and Johnson, Virginia: *Human Sexual Inadequacy*, Little, Brown, Boston, 1970.

Mayleas, Davidyne: *Rewedded Bliss*, Basic Books, New York, 1977.

Mead, Margaret: "A Continuing Dialogue on Marriage: Why Just Living Together Won't Work," *Redbook*, April 1968, pp. 44, 46, 48, 50-51, 119.

Meriwether, Elizabeth: *How to Win and Hold a Husband*, Doubleday, Doran and Co., 1939.

Napolitane, Catherine with Pelligrino, Victoria: *Living and Loving after Divorce*, Signet Books, New York, 1978.

National Center for Health Statistics: Advance report, final mortality statistics, 1980. Monthly Vital Statistics Report, Vol 32-No. 4, Supp. DHHS Pub. No. (PHS) 83-1120. Public Health Service, Hyattsville, MD, August, 1983.

National Center for Health Statistics: Annual summary of births, deaths, marriages, and divorces: United States, 1982. Monthly Vital Statistics Report, Vol. 31, No. 13, DHHS Pub. No. (PHS) 83-1120, Public Health Service, Hyattsville, MD, October, 1983.

Neubeck, Gerhard. "In Praise of Marriage," *Family Coordinator* 28, (January 1979), 115-117.

Novak, William: *The Great American Man Shortage*, Rawson Assoc., 1983.

Pearlin, Leonard and Johnson, Joyce: "Marital Status, Life Strains and Depression," *American Sociological Review*, 42 (10/77) 704-715.

Perutz, Kathrin: *Marriage is Hell*, Wm. Morrow and Co., Inc., New York, 1972.

Povan-Langston, Deborah: *Living with Herpes*, Doubleday, Garden City, New York, 1983.

Reingold, Carmel Berman: *How to Be Happy if You Marry Again*, Harper and Row, New York, 1976.

Robertson, Nan: "Single Women over 30: Where Are the Men Worthy of Us?", *New York Times*, July 14, 1978, p. A12.

Rubin, Jerry and Leonard, Mimi: *The War Between the Sheets*, Richard Marken Pub., New York, 1981.

Schickel, Richard: *Singled Out*, The Viking Press, New York, 1981.

Seaman, Barbara: *Free and Female: The Sex Life of the Contemporary Woman*, Coward, McCann and Geoghegan, New York, 1972.

Simenauer, Jacqueline and Carroll, David: *Singles*, Simon and Schuster, New York, 1982.

Staples, Robert: *The World of Black Singles*, Greenwood Press, Westport, CT, 1981.

Stewart, Marjabelle Young, *Getting Married Again*, Avon Books, New York, 1980.

Taylor, April: *Love is a Four Letter Word*, Beechhurst, New York, 1948.

U.S. Bureau of the Census, Current Population Reports, series P-20, No. 381, *Household and Family Characteristics, March 1982*, U.S. Government Printing Office, Washington, D.C., 1983.

U.S. Bureau of the Census, Current Population Reports, series P-20, No. 380, *Marital Status and Living Arrangements: March 1982*, U.S. Government Printing Office, Washington, D.C., 1983.

Weber, Eric: *How to Pick Up Girls*, Symphony Press, Tenafly, NJ, 1970.

Weiss, Robert S., *Going It Alone*, Basic Books, Inc., New York, 1979.

Westhoff, Leslie: *The Second Time Around*, The Viking Press, New York, 1977.

Index

Gambling, compulsive, 137
Grooming, 49-59, 104
Groups
  adjustment, 12
  of recently divorced, 12
  therapeutic, 3, 11-12
Group therapy. *See* Psychotherapy
Guidelines
  for dating, 116-17
  for dieting, 36-38
  for finding the right man, 158-59
  for meeting men, 83-84
  for singles bars, 73

Hair
  care of, 44-45
  excess, 45
Health
  and being single, 166
  disease, 98-99, 118-19
  marriage improves, 19
  menopause, 38
  mental. *See* Psychotherapy
  physical examination, 52
  and post-divorce and widowhood,
    10, 148
Home, location and decorating, 52-53
Homosexuality, 134
Humor, 151-52
Husband-finding
  and available men, 61, 69, 71
  and choosing a mate, 127-60
  and competing with other women,
    62
  and dealing with prejudices, 63
  "feminine" methods of, 5
  and getting married, 147-48
  and job change, 72
  and ways to meet men, 69-73

Image
  appearance, 33-52
  entertaining, 48

home, 52-53
Impotence, 95-96

Jealousy, 137
Jewish Family Services referrals, 12
Jobs
  changing, 72
  and child care considerations, 59
  and the healthy mental attitude, 56
  and the mentor, 65
  relating household skills to, 9, 56
  and suggested fields to choose from,
    58-59
  where to look for, 57

Lingerie, 48-49
Living together, 151, 153-54
Loneliness
  coping with, 23-26, 28-29
  and decision making, 62
  definition of, 27
  feelings about, 9.
  See also Adjustment groups
Love
  and marriage, 144-45
  as a reason to marry, 143
  romantic, 142
  and second marriage, 169
  and security, 145

Mail-order brides, 107-8
Makeup, 42, 44
Male chauvinist pig, 133
Man
  finding the right, summary, 158-60
  women's definition of, 126
Marriage
  attitudes of the 1950s, 2
  and being asked, 154-58
  case stories of, 13-15
  comments in favor of, 165-66
  current and future trends of, 29-31

evaluation of what went wrong, 16-
  18
and the five Cs,31
and love, 144-45
negative comments on, 165
and younger men, 64
Married men, dating, 67
Matchmaking, 70, 78.
  See also Meeting single men
Meeting single men
  through dating services, 78, 79
  through gyms, coed, 40
  through matchmaking, 70, 78
  through personal ads, 75-78
  through personal introductions, 69-
    70
  at work, 70
Men
  flaws of, 129-30
  and identity crises, 30
  improved by marriage, 167
  and meeting available women, 68-69
  older, 65, 88
  and overweight women, 34
  qualities of, 126-27, 129
  and sexual problems, 95
  shortage of, 22-23, 29, 82
  traditional, 128
  types of, 127
  and women in middle years, 3.
  See also Men to avoid
Menopause, 36, 38
Mental health. *See* Psychotherapy
Men to avoid
  always swinging single, 134
  the bossy bull, 138
  the bully, 141-42
  the cheapskate, 140-41
  the eternal youth, 139
  the gold digger, 142
  the golden glove kid, 133
  the hypochondriac, 139
  the male chauvinist pig, 133
  Mr. Fixed, 133
  Mommy's little darling, 133-34

the neurotic, 140
with sexual problems, 134
the spendthrift, 141
the tin man, 133
the workaholic, 138
who worships women, 134
Mentor, 65
Money
  accepting, 151
  and the cheapskate, 140-41
  and credit cards, 55-56
  and entertaining, 24-25
  and first family, 153
  and the gold digger, 142
  handling, 54-55
  and prenuptial contracts, 177
  and the spendthrift, 141

Overeaters Anonymous, 36

Parents Without Partners, 121
Personal ads, 75-78. *See also* Meeting
    single men
Personality
  changes in, 129
  traits, 130-31
Physical abuse, 141-42
Plastic surgery, 45-46
Pregnancy, 97, 169
Premarital sex, 152
Prenuptial contracts, 177
Professional help. *See* Psychotherapy
Proposals, 156-58
Protestant Family Services referrals, 12
Psychotherapy
  to face divorce, 3
  and group therapy, 11-12
  and illness and depression, 11
  and low-cost help, 12
  results of, 129
  and self-destructive cycles, 11.
  See also Adjustment groups